LOVE IS PATIENT

A Christian Romance

Love Is
Book 1

FAITH ARCENEAUX

Copyright © 2023 by Faith Arceneaux

All rights reserved.

No part of this book may be reproduced in any form or by any electronic or mechanical means, including information storage and retrieval systems, without written permission from the author, except for the use of brief quotations in a book review.

❀ Created with Vellum

To my ARC readers, thank you for joining me on this journey.

Newsletter

I pray this story will inspire you, and at the least entertain you.

If you love it, and want to be the first to hear about the next release, join my newsletter.

Join Here: https://bit.ly/faith2love

Chapter One

MORGAN

"Dear God, please give me the strength to get through this day." As I looked at the shards of broken glass on the dresser, I laughed at the thought of God peering down at me and saying, "New number who dis?" It'd been that long since I last called out to him.

But I hoped He would still answer.

Because if the state of my house was any indication of how my life was, it was torn to pieces. And I needed Him to help me piece it back together.

The night before was the worst it had ever been with Elijah. But it wasn't the first time he'd come home in a fit of anger misdirected at me.

The clock blinked 11:37 as I heard the front door creak open, well past the time he'd usually come home. Lying in bed, I anticipated the worst. There could only be two reasons he was home that late—he was out celebrating his promotion and had gotten drunk; or he didn't get the promotion, and he was out drowning his sorrows in alcohol. Either way, neither ended well for us. Certainly not me.

I listened as his feet stomped through the house, pausing in the living room where I'd usually be waiting for him. Then his voice, booming, as he shouted out for me. His voice echoing off the walls, alerting me, and probably our neighbors whose walls were connected. They were always privy to our world—the glorious and the downright ugly. Whether they wanted to be or not.

His voice only grew louder as he continued through the house, the sound of objects crashing against the wall erected my body against the headboard, the covers pulled up to my neck, as he made his way to me.

Then he found me, his eyes gliding from the top of my head down to my lap before a grimace took over his face. It must have been the sight of my comfort, my seemingly peaceful night that sent him over the edge, because when our eyes connected again, his darkened. The scowl I noticed when he stormed through the door deepened and he flung the covers off the bed. The sudden chill in the air caused my body to shiver. Or maybe it was the way he examined me that made the edge of my nerves vibrate.

His finger flew into my face, as if I was the manager who denied him, and he yelled, "Do you know they had the audacity to tell me I wasn't ready for this promotion?"

The whispered, "I'm sorry, Elijah," went unheard because he was still yelling at the top of his lungs as I climbed from the bed away from his flailing arms.

"And yet, that young dude who just started a year ago is?" He flung a pillow to the ground next like he was in search of something.

I offered to help him find it, hoping his tirade would end, or at least calm down, but that only enraged him more. His stare found mine and he said, "But you probably don't care because you can't relate." I did care. Anything that concerned him, especially that which disturbed him, disturbed me too. Except there wasn't a single word in my vast vocabulary that would have proved that to him. Not in that moment.

I felt air whoosh past my ear, and an object crashed against the wall beside my head, sending shards of glass on the dresser where I stood, only missing my face by inches. "Elijah." I turned and eyed him cautiously. "You need to calm down."

Except calm was the last thing on his agenda for the night. In fact, he became a storm, ravaging through anything in his sight until he reached my side of the room. My breath hitching as the heat from his body pricked my skin.

I stood, staring at him, waiting on him to tell me how somehow my success at work was his downfall. How me working hard, and being rewarded for it, caused him to make poor decisions on his job. How my stellar performance decreased his ability to shine. That was always his argument. Always his line of defense against anything I could offer him in compassion.

It was like watching a maddened dog as he caged me in. Spit flinging from his lips as he told me, "It wouldn't faze you one way or the other if I got a promotion because you are good."

The rationale didn't make sense. Because in the ten years since we'd been together, the only thing I wanted was to build with him. To create a bond that was unbreakable, pour love that could withstand any doubt, nurture our relationship so that one day we could expand that to our kids.

I believed he wanted that too.

Until I felt his hand grip my chin. His mouth dangerously close to mine when he growled, "You've always thought you were better than me." Then before I could snatch away from his grip, his hand dropped, and I thought he was done. I thought he'd retreat to the other side of the room and whisper an apology. Regret that often found him when he pushed a little too far—when the words he spoke pierced even deeper than he intended.

It was the agony that gripped him that let me know he didn't mean to hurt me. That despite the way his words penetrated my inner being, I trusted that would be it. Only words. And if it was just words, I could withstand his vitriol as long as he never hit me.

Then he did. His hand reached back behind him, and the force of his palm against my cheek darkened my eyes, producing a stream of tears. "Now you want to cry?" His hands gripped my wrist, and the stinging in my face wouldn't allow me to fight back, to jerk myself from his hold. "This is all because of you."

Maybe it was those words, indicative of something I heard when I was younger, that allowed my eyes to open, my chest to rise, and my fear to subside. I rallied my voice and told him, "Get out," in a thunderous voice. One that surprised even me as I heard it.

And I didn't stop repeating it until his hands released mine and he was backing away from me. "Get out, now," I screamed.

The drawers where he pulled his clothes still lay open that morning. The shoes he couldn't hold in his hands as he ran from the house were thrown across the floor. The broken

Love is Patient

glass I tiptoed past as I made my way to the bathroom didn't reflect the picture it once held.

The beautiful picture of him and me—a time when we were happy, whole, madly in love—it wasn't even tattered.

But the two people in it were destroyed.

I looked into the mirror and wept, "God," as I looked at the bruise on my cheek. I reached up to touch my face and remembered the sore spots on my arms, bruises proving how far Elijah went.

I wiped my face and took a deep inhale as I considered what was next. In all the years I spent with Elijah, leaving him, breaking up, being apart was never a thought that crossed my mind.

It wasn't like I didn't know back then when his words were his sword, that one day he'd escalate. I'd seen it before. Too many times in fact. And then, I vowed to myself that I'd never allow it. I'd never be like my mama, letting men talk to her any type of way. Hurting her while she apologized for making *them* angry.

I wasn't supposed to fall for *that* guy. The one she'd parade in front of us after the last left her high and dry, beaten and broken.

With a trembling hand and a shake of my head, I made myself the same promise I made back then, "It won't be me. I won't allow it." I was convinced me and Elijah were done. No matter how much he tried, I wouldn't let him back in my life.

That was a start. And with the blaring alarm going off in the bedroom, I was reminded of what he hated most about me. A successful job. I had to get to work. With bruises on my face and arms, hours of restlessness, I needed to show up. I could only imagine, wherever Elijah was, he allowed himself the leisure of sleeping in. Rolling over and turning off his alarm, justifying his absence for the day with a shake of his throbbing head.

I peeled out of my clothes and stepped under a stream of warm water. Carefully showering, allowing the cascade of water to comfort me. It wasn't long before the dam of tears broke, and the shower head wasn't the only thing supplying my body with a deep cleanse.

I wiped the towel gently over my body, not allowing it to linger too long on the pain. And when I felt I could face the day, I stepped out of the warmth of the shower.

Back in front of the foggy mirror, the evidence wasn't clear, but I knew I'd need expert makeup skills to hide the remnants of Elijah's flames. Lucky for me, I had years of experience doing just that. Mama would come into our room and ask me and my sister to help her hide the destruction left by the angered man from the night before. Between the two of us, we were able to hide the evidence of hands that should have never graced her body. Not in that way.

She'd examine herself in the mirror when we were all done, and a small smile would escape as she'd commend us for another job well done. "Perfect," she'd say as she fluffed her curls and stood from our bed. But it wasn't perfect. Far from it in fact.

No amount of makeup could hide the scars that were etching themselves in our souls each time we had to perform miracles.

I dabbed my foundation over the concealer, as a tear threatened to undo the artistry. I wouldn't dare whisper, "Perfect," not for a bandage that had been ripped from the scars I had meticulously covered years ago. Not for the eyes that stared back at me swollen, and still red from all the tears I shed.

But I took a deep breath, and again, I whispered, "Dear God, please give me strength to get through this day."

My drive to work was quiet, unlike other mornings when I'd be blasting music, singing along as I made the short commute to the office. The silence so loud, the hum of my car almost lulled me to sleep as I sat at the red light.

The blaring horn behind me made me question if God heard me. If He was listening or if He'd tuned me out because of my lack of contact with Him over the years. I blinked several times as I pulled off in the direction of the nearest coffee shop. *Maybe God's strength was disguised in caffeine.*

I shouldn't have expected the coffee shop to be empty, but the rush of men and women, years younger than me, filing in and out reminded me that I was close to campus, and it was the first day of school.

Their smiling faces and cheerful laughs shouldn't have reminded me of Elijah, but they did. It was the coffee shop we frequented as students ourselves. The strong smell of coffee beans reminded me of our late nights, after studying, when we'd meet up there and spend hours talking.

I shook that off as I reached my arm across the counter to pay for my cup of *strength*. The bruise on my wrist threatening to escape the cardigan I was forced to wear despite the scorching temperatures outside.

That morning I prayed more than I could remember in the past year alone, but still, I adjusted my sunglasses and whispered a longer prayer in case the short and sweet ones weren't as effective. "Dear God, I know that you are a caring God. Forgive me for not talking to you, for not leaning on you, for allowing myself to be ripped from you. Thank you for protecting me from him." As a tear trickled down my cheek, I finished, "Grant me mercy and grace, solace in this storm. Amen."

Chapter Two

CODY

I might as well have laid out my outfit on the bed. Like I did on my first days of school as a kid. That's just how excited I was. If what I was feeling buzzing through my body could have been considered excitement. It could have easily been labeled as nervous energy, anxiety, or the fear of making a complete fool of myself in front of the people I admired the most.

Instead of placing my slacks, shirt, and blazer on the edge of my bed the night before, I spent the night reviewing my notes. Digging through the carefully curated syllabus. Reviewing the profiles of my colleagues to ensure I'd have speaking points if I ran into them in the building between classes.

That went on well into the night, much later than I would have stayed awake on any other night. And the next morning, I was dragging but I was ready to start the day.

So, when my phone buzzed with a call, I was eager to answer it. Even if it meant I'd have to endure the banter from my best friend. He was aware of the day, and despite speaking the words, I knew he was as glad as I was that I was back on the East Coast—only miles from where he resided.

His voice rumbled through the phone as he asked, "You ready for this, man?"

As I responded, my shoulders slumped while I admitted, "Man, what if it's not the same?"

He scoffed, and I heard the roaring of his engine as he said, "Let's hope not. Imagine campus not changing after a decade." Then his relentless tirade about the administration took flight. "I know they don't always do what they need to do with our donations, but shoot. Imagine if it is still the same."

I realized what he was imagining wasn't what I was considering. I knew campus would be different. I'd seen that for myself, not only in the visit I took during the interview, but also as I spent the past couple of weeks organizing my office and meeting with the faculty of our department. "That's not what I meant," I told him.

"Oh, then what do you mean?"

Four years I walked the campus of A&T, back then I was buried in the books, or deep in the code, hidden behind my computer screen. I didn't enjoy college life like most of the guys I hung around. Going to parties was rare, and rotating women through my bed was uncommon. Still, I was indebted to the school that made me who I was. Returning to my alma mater had been a dream since the day I stepped on campus ten years before.

When I started college, I imagined I would join some technology start-up, and use my coding skills to create the next best thing. Prove myself to be amongst the greats like Jobs, Gates, and Zuckerberg. Then like a veil was lifted from my eyes, I realized technology was killing social interactions. And I didn't want to be a part of that problem. I wanted to solve that problem. The best way to do that was in the classroom, issuing a warning to the kids who were just like me, wanting to offer the world another technical solution.

Still, I went on to graduate school, in a different city. Learning even more about technology, but also about the mind. When I graduated again, A&T wasn't amongst my offers to teach. I found myself on a prestigious white campus across the country. As much as I tried to build an affinity with the faculty, setup roots in the city, I could never get comfortable. In fact, returning to A&T became an unwavering desire —something was calling me back to campus and I wanted to be there.

But what if I was mistaken? What if it wasn't the campus I was missing? What if stepping into the classroom didn't give me the relief I was searching for? I looked down at the syllabus for my first class of the day and told Matthew, "What if it isn't what I've been hoping for all these years? The classroom, the students, the faculty." In my mind, returning would feel like the coveted homecoming I returned to every year in the fall; it'd feel like a warm embrace by my mama; a pat on the back from my dad; a bright smile from a beautiful woman. I wanted that belonging to course through my blood as I stood across from students whose faces mirrored mine. "What if I still can't get settled here?"

Matthew groaned on the other end. "Here we go with this existential crisis you seem to be facing every couple of months." His gruffy laugh bellowed into the phone before he told me, "Listen, you're still in your thirties man, you aren't supposed to be hitting a midlife crisis yet. And definitely not every couple of months."

I wagged my head because I guess what I feared did sound something like a midlife crisis. It did sound like I was running to and from the same thing, and therefore found myself in a circle that was never ending.

But when Matthew declared, "I'm telling you, being back on campus, I'm sure your odds of finding a woman to take your mind off all of that have increased." He reminded me, "You'll have all shades of brown, brilliant women, gorgeous women, athletic women, women with goals—"

"Man, listen, I'm not trying to be *that* professor." I groaned at the thought of dating a student as Matthew defended his remarks.

"Last I checked, there are faculty members, other professors, staff. Teacher's assistants, graduate students that don't really count as undergrad students." Then he smacked his lips and said, "You know what, how soon can I make a visit?" We both laughed and before solidifying any plans, he told me, "I better run, my first patient for the day will be here soon and I'm still sitting in my car in front of the building."

"Alright, I'll catch up with you later," I said as I grabbed all my papers and shuffled them into my bag.

I didn't want to be late on my first day, and the way my energy was already starting to wane I'd need a little boost to make sure I was ready for my first class. I looked around my apartment at the unpacked boxes and sighed—my coffee machine was buried in one of them.

I needed to get settled in, make the place feel like home, and not the college dorm that went undecorated for four years. Or the places I stayed in for graduate school, and even as a professor in California.

Moving back to Greensboro meant I was going to settle in, make myself comfortable, and welcome everything God had to offer with me moving back. I could only hope that would finally be a chance at love. Something I'd been missing out on for most of my adult life.

If not for me, it'd at least answer one of my mama's recurring prayers.

I took the elevator down to the parking garage and climbed into my car. The drive to campus was short, and when I stopped in front of the coffee shop, I watched students shuffling inside. The idea of being in that same coffee shop a decade prior brought a smile to my face. I spent countless hours there, emptied cups of coffee in front of me as I buried myself in my books, or whatever project I was working on.

The walkway leading up to the front door gave me time to appreciate the full circle moment. Although I wasn't *home*, opening the front door of the shop made me feel like I'd been welcomed by my mama's smiling face inside.

And that's exactly what I got walking in through the door. Familiarity engulfed me and eased whatever nervous energy was firing through me earlier that morning.

I joined the back of the line and looked around. Not much had changed with the shop, certainly not the aroma of coffee beans, the soft music playing in the background, and the students occupying the tables. Even the long line, extending to the front door, was still the same.

The biggest difference was all the phones that were clenched in the hands of the people gathered in the shop. Instead of casual conversations, I saw eyes focused on the screens, constant scrolling, and few conversations. I shook my head as I approached the counter to order. "I'll have a coffee with cream and sugar." A simple enough order that was met with wide eyes.

"Just regular cream and regular sugar?" I laughed and nodded. "I guess," the young woman sighed before I paid. I moved to the side and made it a point to take in all the people around me. To watch the interactions between the students at a table nearby. The faces as people rushed in and left out in the same hurry.

"Morgan," I heard the woman behind the counter shout a couple of times. The woman standing in front of the me, the only other person waiting on an order, didn't move. I stepped beside her, and as my eyes met hers I shook my head.

"Can't be," I whispered.

The one thing I didn't factor into my return to campus was running into anyone I'd known previously. Sure, there were still some of the same professors, faculty, and staff that had been there when I was a student. And that was half of the appeal of going back, to work alongside the people who molded me. To be amongst the educators I admired the most.

But running into a familiar face, one of my peers from years prior, wasn't anything that had crossed my mind.

And maybe it should have been, because seeing her was like my mama's Sunday dinner—it comforted me deep down on the inside. Seeing *Morgan* touched my soul.

Chapter Three

MORGAN

Somewhere between ordering my coffee and waiting, I slipped into replaying the events of the night.

Elijah's footsteps as he stomped through the house, his voice that echoed against the walls, and the piercing sound of glass shattering. The words he shouted were clear in my mind. I could have recited them as a mantra the way they looped through my thoughts. Each iteration making me more and more tense.

"Morgan?" I had just adjusted my glasses to look at the woman calling my name, when another voice repeated it.

"Yes?" I looked into his face and blinked. My mind was having difficulty shuffling through the memories as it was bombarded of thoughts of the night. But his face. It was familiar. His voice too. The way he looked at me, his eyes narrowed, and a warm smile covered his face. I looked away and tried to grab my coffee.

If he was someone who remembered me, I didn't want him to see me like that. How I was standing there with swollen eyes, a bruised body, and a shattered heart.

But he didn't waver even as I tried to avoid his gaze. "Morgan Moore?" He stepped in front of my line of sight as he handed me the coveted cup of *strength* I needed to make it through the day.

"That's me. Thank you." Although mentally I knew I should smile, that my lips should curve upward as I graciously grabbed the cup from his hand, I couldn't.

Not a muscle in my face wanted to cooperate with the signal from my brain to *smile*. Such a simple request was denied upon request. Rejected without explanation, rebuffed without an alternative suggestion. I stood stone faced, willing myself to not cry in front of the man who seemingly knew me as my mind fought the memories of the night, to search for the memory of his face. Of his voice.

"I can't believe it." He stepped to the side, and I instinctively followed. "It's been years since the last time I saw you." His memory was recalling the last time, as mine was trying to remember the first time. *Where do I know you from?*

As his smile up ticked, something sending an instant wave of jealousy to me as physically my body was still on strike, he said, "You don't remember me, do you?" An apology was on the tip of my tongue when he said, "Cody. Cody Felix." He explained, "We were here on campus together."

His reminder, the time and the place, was able to issue a silencing effect to my mind. Allowing me to recall the man standing before me, during a time that wasn't lost with me. "Cody Felix." I couldn't help the gaze my eyes took over his face, down his body, and back up to his beaming eyes.

My mind didn't recall him easily because years ago, *Cody*

Felix didn't look like the man standing before me. The man standing before me was easily one of the finest men I'd ever seen. Including the man I wanted to forget I'd ever known. Cody Felix was like the cup of coffee I gripped in my hands, dark, smooth, and energizing. His body wasn't the same lanky body it was when I'd seen him on campus all those years ago. The baby face was replaced with a beard that framed his defined jaw line and eyes that were warm and *mature*. I tilted my head to the side and asked, "What are you doing here?" in a tone that wasn't intended, without a smile that I couldn't conjure. The flash of pain I saw in his eyes, I regretted immediately. "Sorry." I took a deep breath as I held up my free hand.

His eyes went down to my wrist, and I quickly moved it back to my side before he could see the reason why a smile was so difficult to form across my face. "Today's my first day of school." He beamed with pride. "I'm back here teaching."

I made the connection and nodded. Before I turned to leave the coffee shop, I told him, "Well, welcome back." Anyone else observing us would have likely thought my statement wasn't sincere or genuine because my appearance lacked the warmth I felt inside as I stated it. But I had to move before he asked me any questions—about me, and my life, about the person he knew I was with back then.

As I walked out of the coffee shop, I sipped the coffee and took a deep breath. If I was going to make it through the day I'd likely need to avoid anyone who knew me. Especially if they'd look at me the way Cody Felix looked at me—like he knew the lies I'd tell him if he asked if I was okay.

I walked into the Law Offices of Jakobi & Sutherland, with a straight back and determination to make it to my cubicle before anyone who knew me well could intercept me.

It'd only be a short retreat as one of the lawyers would be on me soon enough with their requests of the day.

Still, I sat behind my computer and eased my sunglasses off my face, hoping they'd leave anything that could have been an email, well, an email. Before my computer illuminated, I spotted my reflection in the black screen—somber, disheveled, and tired.

Being at work acting like nothing was wrong was a skill I acquired over the years. It wasn't just the fact that my relationship with Elijah went from bad to worse, and that many nights we argued and fought until I had no more energy to argue. It was the fact that being a paralegal wasn't what I wanted.

It paid my bills, and allowed me to maintain a decent lifestyle, but despite Elijah's thoughts around me being happy and successful at work, it wasn't what fed my soul.

All my life I was a dancer. Expressing my emotions through flawless movement. Transferring my hopes to the audience with pliés, grande jetés, and sissonnes.

Sitting behind a desk, researching cases, and drafting briefs wasn't exactly fulfilling. But still, when asked how I was doing at work, the answer was always, "I'm doing well." A lie.

So, when I heard someone approaching, I braced myself to repeat the same lie with a different underlying secret. It wasn't just about not being fulfilled in my job, but it was about the tattered way my relationship ended hours prior.

Unfortunately for me, it wasn't just any of the lawyers or other paralegals who leaned against the side of my cubicle, it was Christina. A beautiful Black woman, with an amazing smile and reassuring eyes. Eyes that dared me to lie when she asked, "Good morning, Morgan, how are you?"

I contemplated my response before I admitted, "I've had better days."

She studied my face before I could turn away from her and said, "Hmm. Anything you'd like to talk about?" I shook my head and acted as if the document on my screen needed all my attention. "Alright, well, I'll let you get to it, and we can catch up during lunch."

My heartbeat up ticked as I remembered our long-standing, weekly lunch. As busy as Christina found herself, she always made sure the two of us had a chance to connect outside of the office. Most of the time, our conversations teetered on topics concerning work, but still, it was nice to be outside of the office and at least attempt to talk about anything other than an impending case. "See you then," I said to her as she sauntered away.

Until then, I focused on the brief in front of me. Not the reflection stealing a glance at me with every turn. Not the bruise on my arm reminding me of its pain with every key I typed. Not the agony I felt of returning home that night to the aftermath of the storm that brewed the night before. And mostly not, despite all that, the feeling of being alone in my bed. Of both hating Elijah for what he had become and what he did to us, and still loving him and hoping he'd work it out. Believing that one day he'd be better.

Then, finally, as my phone vibrated across my desk, the realization hit that his better had to be for someone else. I couldn't risk the pain I'd go through waiting for him to be better for me.

The name on the screen, the one that on our best of days would have made me grin with excitement, had a firm scowl on my face as I declined the call and flipped the phone down so that I didn't see any other attempts from him to contact me.

No matter what he had to say, I didn't have room to receive it.

Christina didn't have to remind me it was time for lunch, the loud growls of my stomach did that. I don't know how I expected the coffee for breakfast to satisfy my hunger, or maybe I thought along with my broken heart and fragmented smile, my body would just forget how to function. How to thirst, how to hunger.

It didn't. The louder growl and hunger pains were a reminder that I had to go on. Christina was another, as she said, "Let's go," in the most chipper voice imaginable.

Our walk outside the office with the sun's rays beaming on my neck quickly reminded me that I was wearing a cardigan in the thick of summer. I fanned my face but stopped, and mouthed another lie to Christina as she said, "Take that sweater off," with a chuckle, as if it was that easy.

"Oh, I'm fine. Just trying to block the sun from my face."

Thankfully, she resisted her urge to sit outside on the patio in favor of the air conditioning. We sat across from each other and I zoned into the menu, although we'd frequented the lunch spot many times. I knew exactly what I'd order—the chicken salad sandwich with french fries. The menu was where I avoided Christina's gaze though. I didn't want her questioning looks to attack my resolve.

That didn't last long though. The waiter came to the table and took our orders and collected the menus. The only thing left to do was face Christina.

"Morgan," her voice was quiet as she observed me, "What's really going on?" I introduced Christina to Elijah at one of our work functions; it was a night that should have been light and fun. Drinks were flowing, food was being passed, and the music was even decent. But Elijah quickly found fault in the night, telling me that if I wanted to spend most of the evening chatting with my coworkers I shouldn't have invited him.

Christina overheard that and tried to make light of it, but he wasn't budging. His scowl was sunken, and his arms crossed over his chest like a two-year-old throwing a tantrum. "What makes you think something is going on?" It was a slap to her intelligence, shade thrown on her intuition, but I hoped my question could stall the inevitable conversation we'd need to have about Elijah and everything that happened.

"Well, unless red-rimmed eyes and a pile of makeup on your face is the new trend, then…" She sat back in her chair, but her eyes never left mine. "Did the two of you get into another fight?" Her eyes were narrowed, and I sighed. "Morgan, are you okay?" she pleaded.

I couldn't have been more excited for the waiter to return to the table with our food, giving me a little reprieve from the questioning stare. A moment to decide how I'd proceed.

A mouthful of my sandwich allowed me to formulate the response I wanted to give her. "No, last night was the worst it's ever been. I hardly got any sleep afterward, but I told him to leave."

The admission lightened the weight on my chest, and I blinked at the sudden ease I felt with just telling her he was the cause of my sleepless night. "Oh, Morgan." Her hand eased across the table and caught my wrist before I could move it. My cardigan sliding up as she did, and her eyes landed on the bruise.

The weight, it was back, and much heavier than before. I

could hardly breathe as her eyes pleaded, begging for me to elaborate on what happened between me and Elijah. I softly shook my head, letting her know one more word from my mouth, another look of pity from her would cause the dam to break, and it was the last thing I needed before we had to wrap our lunch and walk back into the office.

She removed her hand from my wrist, and I slid it beneath the table—out of sight, out of mind didn't exactly apply, but I tried.

"Morgan, I promise if you need anything," she started again, "A place to stay, help with a police report, anything…"

None of those options I even considered. Because with my mama, we never left. We stayed right in our little bungalow, and as one guy left, another one came. The cops were never called because she didn't dare admit to the world what was going on behind closed doors.

And although I didn't want to be like her, I wanted more than anything to just turn the page and forget the last one was riddled with chaos.

I shook my head. "Thank you, but right now, I just want to make it through the rest of the day without tears ruining my makeup." Then as if the mention of the makeup, my face, was a clue to a riddle she was trying to solve, she examined my face.

She didn't have to confirm. The look of her eyes closing for longer than a blink and her chest rising was enough for me to know just how bad the night had gotten. "Okay," she said when her eyes finally opened. "Okay."

I mouthed, "Thank you," as I let my gaze fall back to my sandwich.

I was no longer hungry, but I did feel like I'd need more

strength to make it through the rest of the day. I signaled the waiter, then asked, "Could I grab a cup of coffee to go?"

With the hot cup of coffee in my hand, we walked back to the office. The cup was on my lips and the aroma, the warmth reminded me of the only bright spot of that morning, seeing Cody Felix at the coffee shop. Although my mouth still couldn't form a smile, I felt a tiny piece of my shattered heart restore.

Chapter Four

CODY

 Morgan Moore. I wasn't great with faces or names, but her face and her name was one that was etched into my memory. Watching her walk out of the coffee shop, I could even remember how we met. English class freshman year.
 English wasn't my favorite subject, and even less in college as I tried to spend as much time as possible learning everything I could about computer science. English felt like an unnecessary evil standing in the way of what I wanted to do. Admittedly, I was sitting in the back of the class disinterested in anything the teacher was going to tell us about what we had to look forward to that semester. She was in the middle of reviewing the syllabus when she was interrupted by an opening door, and a girl rushing in to find a seat, any seat. And the only one available was right next to me.
 She took the seat, with a bright smile on her face despite the fact she was obviously late, and the teacher stopped her overview to remind the class, "On time means in your seat before I start speaking." It wasn't her words, or how her face

screwed up when she said it that I remembered most, but the wink that Morgan threw my way as she did it.

That class, instead of listening to the papers we'd have to write, and the books we'd need to torture ourselves reading, I was focused on her. At the time, I didn't know her name, but I wanted to. I wanted to know that and everything else about her.

"Black coffee, regular cream, and sugar." The words felt like they were mocking me, and when I looked back at the woman behind the counter I saw the smirk.

"Thanks."

Walking from the coffee shop back to my car, I reminisced on that semester. English 101, and how Morgan defied the teacher's warning and showed up to class late almost every day. And every day she was rocking a wide grin.

In the coffee shop, ten years later, she was not. The smile I'd expect to see on her face no matter what she was facing was missing. Even if she was late to work, I'd imagine, she would have still been smiling.

Maybe the years had gotten to her. Something snatched the simple joy she so proudly rocked every single day that semester.

I had the courage then to ask her after class what her name was, and when she proudly told me, "Morgan Moore," with an outstretched hand, I could almost remember how delicate her fingers felt covered with mine. My courage stopped with asking her name. I didn't have the boldness to ask someone like her to kick it with me after class.

Weeks after that first day, I realized I was too late anyway. There was a dude, I narrowed my eyes as I drove across campus as I tried to remember him, he was waiting outside of English one day and her smile when she saw him was the biggest I'd ever seen. There was a different type of glow in her eyes as she looked at him. Her entire body came alive as his hand enveloped hers and she cozied into his side.

"Elijah," I shouted as I pulled into the parking spot in front of my building. Her voice was soft and whimsical the day she told me about him. It was one of those days when we had to work on a project together. We were huddled in a small corner of the library, and the poem we were analyzing was all about love, or at least that's what she had decided. I was convinced it was about a warm summer's day. But the way she told it, made me realize she felt it differently than I did.

I looked ahead at the building I should have been rushing into but decided to remember that conversation instead. "See," she said, stiffening her back and holding her head up high, "It's the sun's rays," she beamed, "That feeling of warmth as it overcomes your body and chases away the clouds. Reminds you that there is hope, and possibility." I stared at her, admiring what she had said, and considering how she came to that conclusion when the words on the paper said, "The sun's rays pierce the sky." Then she sighed, "It's like when Elijah wraps me in his arms." And I knew then that any chance I thought we could have was over—if she thought of *Elijah* when she read that poem there was no way I'd be able to replace him. Especially not when the breadth of my understanding of love didn't even scrape the cloud the sun's rays chased away.

Shaking my head, I climbed out of my car and rushed into my classroom. To my surprise, it was packed. Every seat filled, and although there was chatter as I approached, all eyes were on me as I stood in front of the classroom.

"Good morning." I made eye contact with each of the

thirty plus people staring back at me. "This semester…" I started and gained enthusiastic nods as I explained the semester's curriculum. When I finished, I asked, "Are a few of you brave enough to explain why you chose to take this course?"

Being a new professor, teaching a new class on a subject that was contrary to their studies had me curious. I knew why I was there, and why I wanted to teach the class. I just wasn't convinced completely about why they were there.

During my studies, if I read the course description I probably would have laughed it away. It would have been like English, unnecessary to accomplishing my goals.

After a long pause, one student raised their hand and said, "I think I've experienced it," she went on to say, "Technology can be a gift and a curse. When real-life experiences are tainted by capturing the moment, instead of living the moment, the moment passes us by."

My face lit up, and I pegged that woman as my star student. I just couldn't let her, or the other students, know that yet. I pointed her way and said, "Absolutely," as I nodded my head emphatically. "Obviously, there are things that technology can gain us, in fields where living without it could be detrimental to our health or well-being," heads were nodding, "Like in the medical field, there have been advancements that have made technology necessary." I laughed and said, "But can we say that dating is any better through an app?" I saw some heads wagging and watched as other's faces contorted. I pointed, "Okay, so now I'm in your business." The class laughed and I felt even more at ease. Then I warned, "Just so you know, during this class your phones will be forbidden. I expect that you will be here, present, always engaging me and your fellow classmates." I smiled. "I know some things I say may be tweetable, but just do your best to memorize it." I heard a few snickers and challenged, "Oh, you doubt me?" I looked at one guy who had a frown on his face, and I pegged him as the one I'd have to persuade. I was up for the challenge.

By the end of the class, I was convinced I made the right decision to return to A&T. That feeling I wasn't sure I'd get there, was absolutely there.

It was like the sun's rays piercing the sky…

Even as I walked from my class across the quad to my office, seeing the students made my heart swell with pride. I was *home.*

Two students, holding hands as they walked past, reminded me of Morgan again. I imagined the two of them were as inseparable as Morgan and Elijah. Whenever I saw Morgan, I saw Elijah. Even as the years went by, I spotted the two of them randomly across campus, still holding hands. Her smile just as bright as it was that first day I saw her, and even brighter than the first time I saw her with *him.*

"Dr. Felix," I heard a vibrant voice behind me, and I turned. "First class out of the way yet?" I nodded. "And how'd it go?" One of the professors, Dr. Alicia, as she wanted the students to call her, was a member of our department. And if I remember correctly one of few supporters of my suggested course.

"The students were receptive and even seemed excited." I smiled then joked, "At least until I warned them cell phones weren't permitted in the class."

Her eyes widened. "Bet that'll be a challenge," she said as she snuck her own phone into her pocket. "Headed to your office?" I nodded, and she asked, "Mind if I walk with you?"

"Not at all." She started asking how it felt to be back on

Love is Patient

campus and I noted, "You know," with a smile, "it's better than I expected."

"Oh." Her eyes widened. "That's good to hear. I'm sure the students and faculty," she looked in my direction and her smile widened, "will be happy to know that."

In the four years on campus, there wasn't anyone else that interested me the way Morgan had. And once I started getting into the classes for my major I convinced myself I didn't have time to date anyone.

It wasn't until after undergrad that I took a chance on a few women, but none of the relationships stuck, none of them gave me that feeling that Morgan described that day in the library.

Matthew tried to tell me I missed out on opportunities because I didn't see the obvious way women flirted with me, and I looked at Dr. Alicia and thought, *could she be flirting?* She was pretty, had an amazing smile, and a cool demeanor, but maybe she was just being nice.

I let the moment pass and told her, "I'll see you around," as I stepped into the opened door of my office.

As the sound of her heels against the floor continued down the hallway, I reminded myself that the other reason for me to return to my alma mater was to settle down. To find someone I could build a life with.

I wanted that *hope and possibility* Morgan described.

The notes for my next class were sprawled on my desk. Amongst the proposed class, Technically Social, I was teaching, I also had a few standard computer science courses I was responsible to teach. Those classes wouldn't be as engaging and would likely require more brain power, so I should have been focused.

Still, the only thing I could focus on was Morgan.

Like those first few weeks of English 101, when I could hardly listen to the professor explaining stanzas and sonnets, I couldn't focus on the coding languages or syntax in front of me. I wanted to sit and dream about Morgan—and all the things she'd been doing to occupy her time since I last saw her years prior. I wanted to know why she never left Greensboro when it seemed that was the only thing she could talk about when we met. I wanted to know if she had ever graced the stage in New York, because that was one of her biggest dreams. Or if that love she described back then was still filling her heart.

Laughter filled the hallway in front of my office, and my thoughts flickered to the way hers would fill any space we were in without a care. Especially the library. When we should have been quiet, trying to whisper and not disturb the people around us, her laugh couldn't be silenced. She'd burst out into a fit of giggles, and there wasn't anything I could do or wanted to do to stop her or prevent myself from joining along. She was just that magnetic.

The urge to learn more about the woman she became grew stronger with each passing minute. Unlike back then, I decided, I'd be brave enough to ask her out.

If only I could bump into her again.

Chapter Five

MORGAN

Days had gone by since my fight with Elijah. Although I wasn't back to *normal*, I was finally able to get a few hours of sleep the night before. I didn't realize how much of a hole I'd feel from his absence.

Even though some nights he came in late, we'd spend the night next to each other. His heavy arm resting over my stomach until we both fell asleep, and my head would find its way to his chest—the sound of his heartbeat lulling me into a deep slumber.

Each night without him was a challenge to find that warmth, that thump, the weight of him. I wanted to know that he was there, with me. And the realization that he wasn't made each moment of rest a chase.

No matter how fast I had to run after it, or how deep I had to dig to find it, I was determined I would. One day.

I couldn't give in to the desire to just make things easy

again, to fall back into his arms because I was too afraid to be without him.

It didn't matter much, because his name stopped gracing the screen of my phone. Not in text or a phone call. I started to think what I was feeling was severely misaligned to what he felt for me.

Where I laid awake at night missing him, was he even worried about what I was doing? Or who I was with? Or was he so sure that I was where he left me, and there was no need to even check on me?

I bit the side of my mouth as a notification dinged on my computer letting me know it was time for lunch. I snatched my bag and made my way outside into the warm air. Thankful I was able to finally go to work without a cardigan to hide my bruises, because the sun was beaming again.

The vibrating of my phone stilled my steps, and I dug for it out of my purse. Seeing his name didn't do what I thought it would. I thought my heart would have leaped for joy, but it only sunk in fear as I contemplated even answering his call.

I didn't have to decide because the phone stopped vibrating in my hands. Relieved, I started my trek to the café, then it started vibrating again. "Hello," I answered, holding my breath as I waited for him to speak.

"We need to talk." His voice was deep, firm, and didn't give me any sign that what he wanted to talk about was an apology.

"Elijah, I'm busy," I told him, not wanting to hear anything he had to say.

He barked back, "That's the problem, always too busy for me." He scoffed. "As if I'm not taking time out of *my day* to call you. I'd think the least you could do would be to find a minute to speak to me."

I didn't have a minute, let alone a second to listen to anything he had to say, especially if it didn't start and end with, "I'm sorry." Even then, I determined talking to Elijah wasn't what was best for me. Not the way the tears were threatening to cascade down my face, and my heartbeat was racing, and not in the warm and fuzzy, *I'm excited to speak to you* type of way.

"Oh, nothing to say, huh. Too busy to even give me an explanation." A headache was forming in my temple, and I wanted nothing else than to be done with the conversation, but for some reason I let the phone linger on my ear as he continued. I looked up to the sky, that despite how I felt was still shining bright, and took a deep breath.

I closed my eyes and said, "God, please help me," silently. Or so I thought.

"God," he barked, "What's He going to do for you?"

I pulled the phone from my ear and looked at it. Elijah wasn't always against God and the church. Over the years, as our relationship started to splinter, so did his with God. Or maybe it was his fracture with his relationship with God that caused the turmoil between us. Whatever it was, instead of maintaining what I had with God, I lost faith too.

As a tear fell from my face, I didn't dignify his question with an answer; instead, I hung up. Walking into the café with a tear-stained face was the last thing I needed, but not immediately going in would mean I'd be late to the office, and I didn't need that either. So, I took another wavering breath, wiped my face, and opened the door.

The smiling woman behind the counter should have elicited a smile from me, but instead of smiling, I quickly ordered my food and tried to turn away before she recognized the despair on my face.

Looking around the crowded café for an available table, my eyes landed on him. *Again.* To my surprise, his eyes were on *me*. And he, too, had a wide grin on his face, one I couldn't even plead with myself enough to return.

His subtle head nod for me to join him was met with a turn of my head as I looked for anywhere else to sit. When I found none other, I slowly walked toward him. "You sure?" I asked, standing in front of him.

"Of course." He looked around as if it wasn't a question, even if there was another table available, and said, "Looks like there aren't many options anyway."

"Thanks," I said softly, sliding into the chair across from him.

Our eyes connected before mine faltered, trying to find someplace else to land. The hands in my lap seemed like the best place to stare. "How have you been?"

The question on any other day would have been simple. The most basic way to start a conversation, but that day it was heavy. The reply stuck in my chest because I couldn't tell him I was broken, torn apart, although sitting in front of him a whole person, I was actually a fraction of myself.

Instead of the easy, "I'm well, how are you?" I admitted, "You know," as my eyes met his, "I can remember better days." But I didn't consider he'd want to know more. I thought the icebreaker and rebutted response was enough to end the trajectory into my feelings.

It wasn't.

In fact, the way his face turned into a scowl somewhat matching mine, I was concerned he'd not only want to know exactly why I was not having a good day, but how he himself could resolve it. Cody Felix was that guy. The one I should have dated, not the one I ended up with who couldn't care less if my day was horrible as long as his was going great.

The sigh that left my breath as he said, "That's too bad, anything you want to talk about?" threatened to peel back the bucket of tears that were pooling in the corners of my eyes. "Or," he offered, "we can talk about anything else. Something that'll make you forget about the bad."

"That," I said quickly, "Let's go with that." And I almost felt a laugh building in my chest as he nodded his head.

My sandwich arrived, and he looked across the table and noted, "I was wondering how much had changed with you." I narrowed my eyes as I took my first bite. I didn't have a ton of time for lunch.

"What do you mean?" I asked after I swallowed the first bite and was going in for the second.

He pointed across the table and said, "You ordered that when we would come here after class."

I looked down at the turkey on rye, with mustard and mayo that had been my staple sandwich for as long as I could remember and said, "You remember that?"

The smile he returned let me know he remembered that, and probably more. His eyes were bright with satisfaction as he said, "Oddly, yes." I could have asked to confirm how much he remembered, but staying out of the past and not talking about me, and who I was when he knew me then, was probably for the best.

I asked, "How are you liking being here again, teaching?"

Not once did his warm smile falter as he described the feeling of being back, of being in front of students who he wanted to help more than any others he'd ever been around. "I want to make sure they graduate knowing how they can help the world, and not add to the already existing chaos."

Although I was on my last bite of food, I wanted to know how he felt what he was teaching the students in the classroom could do what he was describing. "How's that?"

His response was passionate, deliberate, intentional, and for a moment, I was lost in it. In the expressions on his face, the animated way he directed my attention around the café, at others who were lost in their phones instead of leaning into the person across from them. "How many opportunities to connect do you think are lost in the moments when they are here deep in their phones," he pointed to me, "instead of here?" The way his eyes stared into mine made me relate to exactly what he was saying.

After all, it was one of the arguments I'd have with Elijah. The time we were together, he wasn't present. Instead of asking me about my day like I was trying to ask him, he was scrolling on his phone.

I wiped the sides of my mouth with my napkin and was preparing to leave when he asked, "What about you? I didn't think you'd still be in Greensboro."

The smile on his face assured me he didn't mean any harm with his words, and the way his head tilted to the side, I believed he was genuinely curious. But telling him that would spring forth the tears that had finally decided to dry up. "I should get going. I need to get back to the office."

The curious smile fell from his face as I stood from the table. "Right. I should too." Then he stood in front of me and asked, "Would you mind if I called you sometime?"

Typically, I'd say, "No, I have a boyfriend," when a guy asked that or something similar. And the words were on the tip of my tongue before I realized that response was no longer valid, or necessary.

I could have easily given Cody my number, could have

even entertained him on the phone. Maybe even let him take me out on a date, or two.

Cody was kind, caring, and sexy.

But when I first met Elijah, he was too.

With my lip worried between my teeth, I shook my head. "I don't think that's a good idea."

The look of disappointment on his face shot an arrow through my heart. I didn't expect to feel bad about turning him down. I'd done it plenty of times before to other men and felt nothing.

Maybe it was because I could have said, "Yes." I could have recited my ten digits as he captured them in his phone. I had every reason to give him my number—I was newly single, and he was a decent guy.

"Alright, well," his smile returned as if my rejection didn't hurt him as much as it did me, and I felt my racing heart slowly returning to normal as he said, "Maybe I'll see you around. Catch you in one of the many places on campus."

I nodded and told him, "Maybe," before leaving him behind in the café.

Chapter Six

CODY

The feel of my feet hitting the trail, my lungs grasping at the next breath, and my mind being clear from any and everything was something I had started to...like. I couldn't say I was in love with running. But I'd grown to enjoy it.

It wasn't something I liked when I was younger, I was more into books than sports growing up. And my body suffered from that as I got older. I had to find something that would keep me in shape and running happened to have a low entry point.

I didn't need any skills, equipment, or even a set schedule. I'd just wake up, lace up my shoes, and get to the closest trail.

That's where I was that morning. The sun wasn't shining when I started, and the air felt half decent. Nothing like my morning runs in California, but I could adjust. Adjust to being in the humid confines of the Carolinas. Although I was sweating within minutes, I still felt that feeling I started to enjoy, my mind focusing on my steps, my breaths, and nothing else.

Maybe that's where my head was when I thumped into something. Or someone. I looked up from the ground and noticed the person stumbling backward. I reached out and grabbed their elbow, as my eyes moved from the ground to their face so that I could look at them when I apologized for not paying attention to my surroundings.

Her flinching eyes caught me off guard. It was Morgan. I'd run into her again—this time literally. But why was she flinching? Her eyes went down to her elbow, where my hand was still gripping, and I quickly removed it. "Sorry." I looked at her elbow. "I wasn't paying attention."

She removed headphones from her ears and said, "It's not your fault, I probably was lost in the music. I didn't notice you." She looked over her shoulders then back to me before the slightest smile crossed her face. "Cody?" I nodded and stepped aside, waiting for her to join me. "Wow, I must have really been distracted. I didn't even realize it was you."

"You know," I said as she looked to be ready to dash off again, "I don't believe in coincidences." Her eyes narrowed and she stayed put as I explained, "Somehow, running into you as much as I have in these last couple of weeks can't be a coincidence. I believe God is somehow orchestrating us being in the same place at the same time." It was something my mama would tell me growing up. That anything I felt was *coincidental* was just God's handiwork in action. I may not have understood it before, but standing in front of Morgan, I felt it. Although I didn't know why it was me and her, in the same place again, especially after I tried and failed to get her number. She apparently wasn't open to what *He* was working out for the two of us. I trusted God had a plan, and if we got out of His way, it'd prevail in the end.

I would have liked to believe after all the years, maybe it was supposed to be me and her. But maybe that would be presuming too much of what God was doing.

"God's handiwork, huh?" There was a smirk on her face, and I couldn't figure out why in that moment that was her response. Why she'd doubt what God was doing, but again, I assumed she wasn't open to finding out. "I should get back to my run."

Mine was ending. The path I was taking was back to my car. I had run the couple of miles I had planned for the day, and somehow, I still asked, "Mind if I join you?"

Her eyes flashed with something I hadn't seen before in her, maybe panic as she looked down at her feet then fiddled with her headphones in her hand. "Okay." She steadied her feet. "Sure. If you can keep up," she teased, and I was relieved that finally, she wasn't rejecting me. Not completely.

The run didn't prove any progress. It was just her and me, together, but essentially alone. She was distracted by music as her legs gracefully ran beside me. I was focused on *her*. I had to be as my lungs were trying to keep up. My body clearly wasn't prepared for another couple of miles, and it was starting to show as we reached our starting point for the second time around. I was hoping she was finished with her run because I was about to tap out. "That's it for me," she said as her feet slowed and she moved her headphones from her ears again.

Her face lacked a smile, but so did mine. The run had gutted me. Before letting the wobbly feeling in my legs and the burning in my lungs get the best of me, I asked, "If you haven't eaten yet, would you like to grab breakfast with me?"

She hesitated, contemplating the idea long enough to make me feel like she hadn't heard me when I said it, so I repeated, "Breakfast?" with a smile.

Finally, she nodded and said, "Where were you thinking?"

Pleased she accepted my offer, I stuttered trying to think of a place to suggest. "How about you pick?" I finally uttered.

"How about Eggselent?"

With a wide grin, I told her, "Sounds excellent." I snickered at my own lame joke, but she just shook her head. "I know, getting pretty bad as I get older."

"Hope you aren't like that in front of the students. I can only imagine their responses."

I assured her, "Not when their grade is involved. You'd think I was a famed comedian the way they force themselves to laugh at me."

As we walked toward the parking lot, I asked, "Where's your car?" She pointed and I followed behind her as she stepped in front of it. I reached my hand out to open her door, and she looked over her shoulder conspicuously. "Just opening the door for you."

"Oh." She nodded. "Right." When she was buckled in her seat, I told her I'd meet her at the café. "Okay, see you there."

I pulled into the parking lot minutes later and questioned whether we should have gone straight from the trail into a restaurant. Even after swiping the sweat from my head, I looked like I dipped in a pool with my clothes on and didn't smell as fresh as I'd like to. But then I looked up from my stained clothes and saw Morgan walking toward the café and hopped out the car. There was no way I was missing out on an opportunity to sit with her. I ran across the street and caught up with her before she reached the door.

"Still able to run? Thought you would have been limping by now."

"She still has jokes, huh?" I said as I opened the door and waited for her to walk inside. "At first my body was rebelling against doubling my normal run, but now I'm feeling like I could go a few more laps." That was a lie, but the way her mouth formed into a little smile, I'd risk telling it a few more times.

"Somehow I doubt that." She winked, and the breath that I was grasping for on the trail was strangling out of my lungs again.

"Table for two," I turned to the hostess and finally said.

Seated across from Morgan, I had a ton of questions pouring into my thoughts. But I didn't want to overwhelm her. I started with, "Do you hit the trail often?"

She wagged her head. "I hadn't in a while, but this morning felt very necessary."

I nodded but wondered without asking what it was that had her needing that feeling. What she was trying to be distracted from. "Not sure what it was that had you out there, but glad I bumped into you."

Her eyebrow peaked. "Quite literally, huh?"

Although her laugh hadn't returned yet, I could see her smile making quick appearances, and I wanted to keep doing whatever it was that made her smile more. "Quite literally," I repeated. "What else did you have planned for your day?"

"Just running some errands," then her face went blank, she shook her head and said, "Then a quiet night at home. What about you?" She looked at the server approaching the table. "Back in Greensboro, what have you found yourself doing around here?"

After ordering our food, I told her, "When I was in school

here, I didn't do a lot. Now, I'm discovering what this place has to offer."

"Maybe if you did a little more before you graduated you would have thought a little harder about returning." She sounded skeptical, like being in Greensboro wasn't her first option.

"Doesn't sound like it's left you impressed."

She hunched her shoulders. "At this point, feels like it's all I know."

"What happened to New York?"

Her eyes flashed from the fork she was stroking to my face. "New York?"

I challenged my memory, trying to think back to our conversation years earlier, and said, "I seem to remember you having this dream to move to New York." I tilted my head to the side. "But maybe I'm not remembering correctly."

She shook her head slightly. "Didn't realize I shared that with you."

I let the moment pass without telling her just how much I remember about her, and the conversations we'd have in the library or the coffee shop. Before Elijah would come in and steal her away.

"I guess I can say life happened. And here I am." Life happened to all of us, and I could understand that.

"And what is that you do now?" I didn't dare tell her I remembered she wanted to be a dancer. Although her body was still shaped like one, I didn't know if that was another dream deferred, and I was trying with all I had to return the smile to her face and not deflate the air from her balloon.

It didn't work. She looked just as deflated when she told me, "I'm a paralegal," with a sigh. I was tempted to ask her what was holding her back. What kept her from going after what she really wanted to do. But the server was tableside again, and the way my stomach was revolting, I needed to dig in.

But first, I reached my hand across the table and asked, "Do you mind if I pray for the food?"

Her eyes looked at my hand as if I hadn't washed them, and I almost snatched it back before she said, "Please," and rested her hand in mine. I watched as her eyes closed with a tilt of her head.

"Dear God, thank you for this food and the hands that prepared it. Thank you for the run we had this morning and allowing us to bump into each other again. Allow this food to be nourishing to our bodies. Amen."

My eyes opened before hers, just in time to see a single tear streaming from her eyes. It felt like a moment I shouldn't have been privileged to witness, so I turned as she grabbed her napkin and quickly dabbed it away. After my first bite, I said, "This is definitely better than the pancakes I would have attempted to make for myself." I hoped that would lighten the mood and rescind any tears that were threatening to fall for her.

"Cody Felix can't cook?" Her eyes widened. "And here I was starting to think there wasn't anything you couldn't do."

I laughed at that. "Stick around, you'd be surprised."

Thankfully, the rest of our meal went more like that and less like knives stabbing into my heart anticipating what had her feeling down.

Our plates were clean, and I wished I had ordered more. Wished I had room for another plate of food, just to extend the time we had with each other. But as I paid, I told her, "Thank you for joining me."

"Thank you for asking." One more question was on the

tip of my tongue, but for whatever reason she declined the first time, I didn't tempt it.

Instead, I told her, "Until the next time we bump into each other."

"Until then," she said with a head nod. "God's handiwork," she repeated as we walked out of the restaurant.

Chapter Seven

MORGAN

When I woke up that morning with a text from Elijah telling me he was ready to pick up the rest of his stuff, I tensed. My entire body felt like it was paralyzed. It took a while before I could even move my fingers across my phone to reply.

But when I did, I told him he could come over that night. I hoped several hours to prepare would get me in the right mindset to see him again. In the same space where everything ended.

It had been years since I hit the running trail, but it felt like the best thing for me to do that morning. To keep my mind off what would happen when Elijah came over. I just needed some time to process everything, and I knew running would do that for me.

I didn't expect to run into Cody, but his smiling face somehow eased the tension I felt in my body. Although I wasn't prepared to be out with anyone that morning, I couldn't refuse his offer. Something about him joining me for my run made me feel safe. From the way he slowed as we neared the second half of the trail, I suspected he was tired, but he didn't give up on me.

In the short period of time we spent together that morning, he reminded me that someone could care. After the years I was with Elijah, I had forgotten that was even possible.

Cody even remembered the dreams I shared in college, the ones I had tucked away and long forgot about. Moving to New York and dancing.

It was Elijah who convinced me that staying in Greensboro with him was better for *us*. For some crazy reason, I believed him.

As his fist pounded on the door, I started to wish that was never the case. I walked toward it and eased it open, feeling my body tense again at the sight of him.

To my surprise, there were no butterflies, no longing, no desire to jump into his arms and kiss his lips like I used to do when we first met. Time didn't seem to erase the hurt I encountered from him weeks prior. Out of sight didn't make me miss him.

"I'm just going to go up and grab my stuff," he said, brushing past me.

I stopped him short of the stairs and said, "No need," as I pointed across the living room, "I packed everything in those boxes."

I'd spent the rest of the day collecting every piece of clothing, shoes, and trinket that belonged to him. I wanted to make sure there was no need for him to ever come back.

That's what would happen with my mom. The men would leave, come collect their stuff over time, then before we knew it the man was back.

I had no room to play that with Elijah. There was no way I was going to let him back into my life. As hard as it was to let go, I had to.

Apparently, Elijah thought otherwise as he screamed, "Oh, you just know we are over, huh?" He pointed at the boxes piled in the corner. "Packed my stuff up just waiting for me to grab it." He stalked across the room and stood in front of them. "Must be another dude that's whispering in your ear making you think you don't need me anymore."

"There was no need for another man to tell me anything." I looked at him with pain in my eyes as I said, "You told me everything I needed to know."

His eyes darkened, and his jaw tensed. With his fists balled at his side, he said, "All of a sudden our little argument is enough for you to leave me?"

I couldn't believe how he was reacting, as if what he did could be minimized to nothing, and without even a half-apology, I'd just be over it. I shook my head and mumbled, "God help me." It had started to be my mantra—recited throughout the day just to make it one more hour.

He ripped a box open and started digging inside. "You want me out of here, that's cool. I'll be out," he said as he shuffled through his clothes. "Just know you'll never find another man who will love you like I did."

My back straightened and clarity that had been missing for weeks returned. "You know what?" He turned from the box and looked at me. "For years I worshipped you, trusted you, believed you." The look in his eyes, the darkened rage was deepening, but I continued anyway, "It should have never been you that I put all my trust in. My hope shouldn't have been in the palm of your hands."

He scoffed as he pushed the box over and crossed the

room to stand in front of me. With his head cocked to the side, he said, "I've been gone a few weeks, and in that time you suddenly found God?" His laugh was mocking, the rage in his eyes replaced with skepticism as he looked at me with a smirk on his face.

Despite the trembling I felt in my hands, I stood in front of him and said, "I've always known Him, but somehow I let you distract me from His goodness." I eyed the boxes and waited for him to retreat, gather his stuff, and get out.

He didn't though. He stood in front of me calling me everything but the name my mama gave me, or a child of God. I listened. I let him hurl every insult he ever considered over the years in my face.

Each word he said lost its power as I heard it. They no longer affected me. I just wanted him out, and when he paused to think of more I said just that, "I think you should leave now."

His hand raised, and I stepped back, making him laugh before dropping it and walking to the other side of the room. "You'll be back. Don't think some other woman wouldn't have taken your place though."

For that woman, I prayed. Prayed she wouldn't be subjected to his harsh words, or his hands. More than anything, I hoped God heard me.

It was a couple of trips to his car before all the boxes were gone, and when he was I quickly closed and locked the door before he could return again. The boxes were gone, and there was nothing left in the house for him.

I grabbed a blanket and curled up on the corner of the couch. I waited for the tears I expected to stream down my face, and when they didn't, I looked around wondering how I was able to make it through all of that without breaking.

Of the many fights I had with Elijah, I didn't share them with those closest to me. Not with my sister, or mom, not even my best friend. It was time though. It was time for me to finally release the protection I thought I owed him. I didn't want them to hate him or treat him differently because I knew he'd still be around.

With no chance of us reconciling, I grabbed my phone and dialed my bestie's number. Ava answered and her voice sounded nothing like how I felt, when she said, "Morgan," with a loud shout, "What's up girl?"

She reminded me that it had been weeks since we had last spoken, but like any other extended break between us, we picked up where we left off. "It has been a minute, and I need to talk to you."

When she replied, "Uh oh," I realized I sounded much more ominous than intended. "You pregnant?"

"Oh gosh, no," I shouted. Then silently, I thanked God that wasn't the case. Just the thought of Elijah with kids frightened me. "Elijah actually just picked up his boxes from the house, we broke up."

"Finally," she shouted, and I paused at her overzealous reaction.

"Uhm," I said, "what?"

She went on to tell me what she really felt about Elijah, and I was surprised she didn't express all that while we were together. I could tell he wasn't her favorite person, but she was talking about him like he was the cause of her little dog's death in elementary school. "Why didn't you ever say anything?"

"What would it have mattered? You were in love." She hesitated, "Unfortunately."

I sunk further down into the couch. "Right." How could I

have loved someone who treated me like dirt on the bottom of his prized shoes? "How'd I let that happen?"

Ava sighed, "I think that's a perfect question for a therapist. Someone who can help you unpack the trauma you've been through. But honestly, Morgan, I'm glad you've decided you deserve better."

"Me too," I said softly. "Just don't know if I'm ready to move on. I think I need some time alone." I joked, "Maybe sit on somebody's couch," then I quickly declared, "Get back into church. Just get back to me, before him."

"I think that's a sound plan." She told me, "Someone who will treat you like the queen you are will appear when you are least expecting it anyway."

I smirked. "Sadly, I'm not sure I'll trust myself to accept it."

"Time," she repeated, "You just need time."

"You're right," I said before telling her, "If all of this hadn't happened, I'd be willing to believe that someone has already appeared."

I could hear the smile spreading on her face. "Do tell."

"Do you remember Cody Felix?" I asked, thinking it wasn't likely because it took me a minute for me to remember him, and I spent a decent amount of time with him freshman year. The crickets on the line were all I needed to try to convince her she knew him. "Okay, the guy I spent a lot of time in the library with freshman year." I continued when she still wasn't responding, "Dark skin, regular guy, not too cute." I contrasted that with how he looked earlier that day. "Now, he's far from regular, and sexy." I let my thoughts linger on his wide smile, and the way his eyes crinkled when he did. The little dimple on the side of his cheek. "Super nice guy." Then I finally said, "The guy Elijah hated."

"Oh," she finally blurted, "Him. That alone should have told us all we needed to know about Elijah. Hated that poor man just because he was being *nice* to you. Like anyone outside of him couldn't just be kind. What'd he used to say, 'He's just trying to smash.'"

"Something like that." I remembered how irate Elijah would get when I told him we'd be in the library together. Then I thought his jealousy was cute, but the way he expressed it should have fired off all types of red flags for me.

"Wait a minute," Ava got eerily quiet before she asked, "I thought he moved somewhere. Heard he was teaching in California at like USC or something."

"I'm not sure about where he was," I admitted, feeling bad for not even asking him where he was before he made it back to Greensboro, "But he's back at A&T now."

"What a coincidence," she sang. *Or God's handiwork.* "And what? You just ran into him randomly?"

Thinking about that day, when I was completely broken after the fight with Elijah and there Cody was, calling my name with his sexy smile. "In the coffee shop," I told her. "One we used to meet at freshman year."

"Wow." She went on telling me that it was more than a coincidence and something worthy of, "Telling the grandbabies."

The thought was crazy, and I let her know, "Except, I just told you. It'll take some time before I can even consider a relationship with anyone." I squirmed under the covers thinking what that would even look like.

"And who says the man won't have patience?" She smacked her lips. "I'm just saying, don't count it out. Seems like it's perfect timing."

"From coincidence to perfect timing, girl, let's talk about

something else." I recalled she had gone out on a few dates the last time we spoke. "How are things with you and the new boo?"

She scoffed. "Over."

"Oh," I said with my mouth hanging open. "But that's a story for another day. I don't even want to get into him and all that drama." She asked, "Besides, I'm checking on my friend who has been radio silent for weeks. Are you okay?"

"Eventually, I think I will be." I believed that fully.

Chapter Eight

CODY

The return to A&T could have easily been credited to a single weekend—homecoming. There was nothing like being on campus the week leading up to the game. After I graduated, I made it a point to return to campus each year for at least that weekend. The fill I got from being around all my friends and the other alumni was enough to satisfy me throughout the year.

Just because I was there permanently, that didn't change. In fact, I even dismissed classes for the Friday before the game, doing for my students what professors did for me when I was on campus—letting them enjoy it fully.

By doing that, it gave me time to welcome my friends as they started rolling into town. Matthew was the first to arrive and eager to prowl the campus. "Man, listen," he told me, "This is the year I need to snatch somebody up because soon, most of the women will be married with kids. Gotta get them before that starts happening." He was seated in the passenger seat of my car as I drove to campus. "I can't wait." He rubbed his hands together.

"Wait," I asked, "Does that mean that you are ready to make one of these ladies your wife?"

He grumbled and turned his eyes out the window. "I didn't say all that." I laughed. "I'm just saying, I need to talk to one before *they* get married."

"Oh, okay." I looked at him sideways as we arrived on campus in front of my building where we could find parking. "Now this trek across campus," I warned, "Maybe you'll see someone along the way." I shrugged, trying to find light in the walk we had to endure.

There was only one person I hoped to bump into. It had been a few weeks since we shared breakfast together and I regretted not trying to get her number again. If I had it maybe I would have been able to invite her out again. Instead, I was scouring every building and path I crossed looking for her.

Except, she was nowhere in sight. I started to think maybe God reconsidered his plan for us.

"Do you remember her?" I felt Matthew's hand on my shoulder. "Over there." He pointed across the street as if there wasn't a sea of people between us and the crowd across the street, and whoever it was he was directing my attention to was like Waldo amongst them. I had no idea who he was referencing.

"I'm going to need more details than that," I said as my eyes scanned the crowd where he was looking. "Who?" My eyes continued a non-committed scan as I tried to find who he could have been talking about.

"Her," he said with even more emphasis.

I didn't know the *her* he was referencing, but I saw the *her* I was looking for. She was standing on the other side of the street and as if the cast of people around her became a backdrop, I saw her clearly. I started across the street as Matthew yelled behind me. "Wait," he called out.

I reached her and didn't take note who she was standing next to. In front of her, I said, "Morgan," loud enough for her to hear me over the crowd, and her mouth grew into the most beautiful smile but faded as quickly as it appeared. "Was starting to think God's handiwork passed us by." I winked.

"Cody," she said softly, but the crowd couldn't do anything to drown out what she was saying. I was intently focused on her mouth, on the words that left it, and anything that had to do with her. From the A&T crop-top shirt she rocked with a ruffled skirt and a pair of sneakers on her feet. She looked like some sort of hip-hop ballerina, and I smiled up at her when I made the connection.

"Dope outfit," I told her with a grin. "What do you have planned for the weekend?"

Before she could respond, Matthew's hand went to my shoulder. "That's her," I heard him trying to say under his breath. I looked over my shoulder to ensure the *her* he was referencing wasn't Morgan, and I saw him staring at the woman beside her.

"Cody, this is my best friend, Ava," Morgan said, and my eyes were on her as if she wasn't trying to introduce me to the woman standing beside her.

Matthew took it upon himself to reach his hand out and shake hers. I could hear their interaction, but I was still focused on Morgan. "Do the two of you have a full weekend planned?"

She wagged her head. "Something like that." I watched her plucking her skirt. "You two hanging out?"

I nodded and told her, "The usual, tailgating, game, maybe a lounge afterward." I would have canceled all those plans if she asked me to, but when she didn't, I told her, "Maybe I'll see you around."

There wasn't a strong tug for me to walk away, but I urged myself to move anyway. "Maybe so," I heard her say as Matthew and I continued the path through campus.

"Cody?" I heard from behind me. "What was that?"

That was God's most beautiful creation. The one woman on earth He could have made just for me. The definition of the sun's rays warming my face. To him I simply said, "Morgan."

He pulled on my shoulder, and as his feet stopped moving so did mine. His head shook back and forth as his arms crossed over his chest. "No, man, what was that between you and *Morgan*?"

My eyes scrunched together, and I looked at his face. "What do you mean?"

He snickered. "Man, listen. That was the most intense exchange between a man and a woman that I've ever seen. And," he paused, "barely anything was said, but everything was understood."

I laughed, rolled my eyes, and tilted my head to the side. "What? You over here talking all smooth. But what are you talking about, really?"

"Just that the two of you seem to have some unspoken chemistry."

I hadn't considered how Morgan felt for me. I couldn't be convinced that everything between us was one-sided, with me carrying all the attraction. For some reason, I was good with that. I was okay if she wasn't feeling me because just being around her brightened my day. I was cool if we just remained friends. After all the years that had passed between us it was comfortable. Still, I explained to Matthew as I convinced him to start walking again, "We met freshman year."

"Okay." He was keeping up with my pace, but may have gotten lost in the reference.

"English 101, and we were cool. I never asked her out, but we worked on projects together, studied together, whatever."

"Then what happened?"

"She had a dude."

"I mean, who didn't freshman year, but did it last?"

"As far as I know, yeah." I explained, "Saw them around campus all four years." I thought back to Elijah again and remembered how much he'd be all over her. Walking hand in hand, and when I'd see the two of them together she'd look away. Alone, she'd speak, but it wasn't like it was freshman year.

"Hmm, well you think they are still together? Didn't see a ring on her finger."

I laughed, remembering his quest to find someone before she got married. "And you were checking for it?"

"Yup, hers and her friends." He slowly let, "Ava," roll from his tongue. "She was gorgeous. They both are. But clearly, Morgan, man or not, I think she might be feeling you." Then he hesitated, "But something seems off."

It was the one thing I noticed the day in the coffee shop, like some of her flame was flickering out. "What do you think it is?" I asked more to myself than to him. I wasn't expecting him to put much thought into what could be wrong with her.

But me, I was trying to do a dissertation on her vibes. Study what made her happy and commit to memory what brought tears to her eyes. I wanted to know what sent her up and always avoid what brought her down.

The smile that quickly faded, I wanted it to stick around, and I wanted to know just how to do that.

"I don't know man, but it's something. Something standing in her way." He noted, "Her friend seemed a little bubblier. But she just looked like she was... existing."

That was it. "And she should be thriving."

"So, what are you going to do, man?"

"I'm going to figure out what happened. In college, freshman year, she was full of life. Vibrant even. Not that woman you just saw back there."

"Bet, and while you do that, if you need help entertaining the friend, I'm your guy." We both laughed.

"Got it."

We finally made it to the other side of campus with a sea of students and alumni all co-mingling and having a good time. As Matthew proclaimed, he was on a hunt for *Miss Right Now*, and I joined him as he talked to women he remembered from our days on campus and alumni he'd never met before. Still, with each introduction, each hug or handshake, there was only one woman I was interested in seeing again.

I prayed, "God, if it's your will, let me connect with Morgan."

There was an evil laugh across from me, and there was something eerily familiar about it. I searched the crowd until I found the person it rang from. *Elijah.*

He was amongst a group of guys and a couple of women.

Not that he was coupled up with any of them, not like he

had been with Morgan on campus when they were inseparable, but that he wasn't with her. If they were still a part of each other's orbits, I would have imagined they would be at homecoming together.

"That was her boyfriend," I said, nudging Matthew, but he was engaged in a conversation with a woman and heard nothing of what I said.

I watched Elijah interact with his friends, the group of people standing around him, and each time he laughed something on the inside of me flipped. Turned. Revolted. I didn't recall not liking the guy back in college, but for some reason, standing there watching him interact without a care, while Morgan was across campus not showing nearly as much excitement, I grew angry.

Mad even.

My fists clenched at my side. Then when his arms wrapped around a woman's neck and he leaned into her ear, I nearly erupted.

It wasn't rational, and I had to rip my eyes away from him and shake my head. *What was it about him that was causing me to be outraged?*

Thankfully, Matthew was ready to continue our trek through the crowd, and I was glad the sound of Elijah's laugh, the sight of his happiness, was behind me.

I continued playing *Where's Morgan* well into the evening, hoping I'd be able to catch her smiling, or laughing, balancing out the anger I felt toward Elijah. I left campus feeling the two opposing emotions—anger and joy.

The last thing I wanted was to let my anger for Elijah shadow my joy. Not again. Not after years of watching him with the woman who was *sunshine's rays* to me. No, I knew there was only one person who could restore my joy, and I hoped He could restore hers too.

God, it's me again, bless Morgan. Let her light shine. Restore her joy. Let the smile that dances across her lips linger long enough for her to feel it in her bones, coursing through her veins, and pumping into her heart. Amen.

Chapter Nine

MORGAN

The sun was shining, the birds were chirping, the laughter of the people walking past me on my way into the office brought a smile to my face. During tough times, it was easy to ignore all of that. The pure beauty in the world diminished because of the sadness within me. It was a like a fog had lifted, and although I was happy it was gone, I was mad that it was even there.

Grew even angrier at the man who was responsible for getting me to that point. It wasn't just the breakup either. Months or even years before that I felt the joy I had slowly fading away. He was sucking the literal life out of me, and I let it happen. So honestly, I was more upset with me.

At me for letting that happen. For not being abundantly aware of the signs that it could happen—before it did. I'd seen it with my mom, on multiple occasions. She'd be the light of any room she walked into, then she'd meet a man, he'd treat her like dirt, and her light would fade. Flicker out like a dull candle.

"No more," that's what I told myself that morning in the mirror. I wouldn't let my light be dimmed for him, for what I lost, or for what I missed out on. I decided from that day forward I was only looking up. Then it happened, I went outside, and it was like I'd been handed a prescription set of glasses after walking around for days without them.

Before I could reach my desk, I peeked in on Christina. She was already in her office and looked busy in front of her computer, a firm scowl set on her brows. "Good morning," I said beaming.

She looked up at me, wide eyes when she saw me staring back. She rose from her desk and quickly stood in front of me. "If it isn't my girl." She wrapped her arms around my shoulders. "I take it today is a better day." She looked at me with slight concern etched into her face, and I felt bad for that. For worrying the people around me.

But I assured her, "Yes," and her smile returned.

"I'm so thankful." She hugged me again. Then she groaned, "I'm super busy, but maybe we can catch up later this afternoon."

I nodded then offered, "Need anything?"

Her fingernail went between her teeth as she said, "Just that brief you are working on, and..."

I laughed, "Coffee?"

Her head went back. "Yes, please."

"I got you. Let me just put my stuff down and I'll run out."

Obviously, it wasn't my job to run out and get her coffee, but it was such a beautiful fall day, I didn't mind prolonging the start of mine in favor of being outside a little longer.

I even took the long route to the coffee shop, walking slowly, noticing the people passing, the cars driving by, and the sounds of nature. *Where was all of this?*

Nearing the coffee shop, I remembered what Cody said the last time we saw each other, at homecoming. Something about thinking God's handiwork passed us by. Then more than ever, I was hoping it hadn't.

Of course, Ava was convinced, maybe I needed to help God out a little and just hand Cody my number. I explained that the opportunity passed, and it'd be hard to just hand it over. Besides that, I was enjoying the random times we bumped into each other.

Easing my way to the front of the line, I hoped that morning would be another one of those random encounters. That God would see fit for Cody to be in the coffee shop, at the exact moment that I was. Then I had to shake my head because that was crazy.

It still didn't stop me from looking over my shoulder after ordering, listening extra hard for his deep voice reciting my name as he did every time he saw me.

I heard, "Morgan," but the voice it was connected to wasn't his. Just the barista with her hands outstretched for me to take the two cups of coffee she was offering.

"Thanks," I said with a bright smile.

The smile was still on my face as I headed back outside. Backing into the door to get out with full hands, I turned to walk up the sidewalk, and I heard my name again.

This time, it was the voice I anticipated. "Morgan," deep and comforting. I turned and smiled. "Wow," escaped his mouth and he moved toward me. "That smile," he noted, "even more beautiful than I remember."

Love is Patient

I tilted my head to the side. "From homecoming?" I asked.

He shook his head. "No, from freshman year."

I felt my cheeks warming but I didn't know why those words created that reaction. "Freshman year?" I repeated.

"Yes," he said, "Although you've kinda smiled these past few times I've seen you," he was staring at me and I realized I was still smiling, "it was never like it was back then. But now, it's back." The smile he had on his face was just as wide, and I tried to imagine what his looked like all those years ago.

I don't know if it was as beautiful, or as wide, if it beamed with joy like it did as I stared at it. But I was glad that I was witnessing it either way.

"I should," I looked down at the cups in my hands, "get back to the office before these get cold."

"Of course," he said, but he was alongside me as I turned away. "Mind if I walk with you?"

I looked to my side and told him, "It's a couple of blocks."

"I have time."

"Okay." I smiled again. "Okay."

He laughed. "How was the rest of your homecoming weekend?"

I thought back to that weekend, and the time spent with Ava, and sighed. "It was good. I needed that time with Ava." Then I admitted, "It was different though." I didn't want to bring up Elijah, but he was the reason it was different. It was the first year I was ever on campus for the festivities and we weren't side-by-side. I couldn't imagine him not being on campus, and the thought of running into him had my nerves in shambles.

Ava made it abundantly clear that she wouldn't bite her

tongue when it came to him, and although I was thankful for her desire to defend me, I knew she was a little firecracker, and he was a match. The two of them arguing would have been explosive.

"Different? In a bad way?" My eyes flashed toward his and I understood why he'd want to know more.

"Not necessarily." We were nearing my building, and I wanted the sidewalk to extend for many more blocks. For the building to move miles away. "What about you?" I hoped his explanation was longer, elaborate, full of words to give me his comforting voice just a little longer.

"It was good." Then he frowned. "I'll admit though, I was hoping I'd see you at least once more, before the game maybe. I would have liked to see what type of outfit you pulled together." He teased, "The hip-hop ballerina look was…" His tongue licked out across his lip, and I don't know if he realized it, but I recognized it and felt something in my stomach flutter. "It was nice."

"Thanks," I said, staring at his mouth as I did. "Well," I said, looking up to the building, wondering why it couldn't have just been a mountain I told to move, "This is my office." I could have just dashed through the opening door, left him there on the sidewalk, but I lingered.

"Hey," he said, and I waited to hear what he would say next, "Would you mind if," he hesitated, even stumbled over his words before he finally asked, "Can I take you out on a date?"

The word ricocheted in my ears, bouncing around like a bullet without a target. "Date?" Of course, the idea wasn't foreign to me, I'd been on dates before. But with someone other than Elijah, I could hardly remember the last time.

Then there was the fact that I wasn't ready to start *dating* again. I felt like I needed more time to myself.

"Yes, a date." His lips curved up into a smile. "Or we can just, you know," he laughed, "take our chances at another run in."

Say yes, was what stopped the ricocheting in my ears. So, I did. "I'd like to go out with you."

I don't know what his smile was before that moment because the look on his face when he heard my response was worth a million dollars. It was like his face was bursting with light particles, his eyes were shining, and his smile was as wide as his face. He wiped a hand across his mouth before asking, "So maybe you can give me your number and we can make plans?"

"Right." I nodded. "Of course." Then I repeated my number for him after he pulled his phone out.

"Got it," he said, staring me in the eyes.

I was hoping he turned first, and when he didn't, I said, "Talk to you later." He held the door open for me, and as I made my way to the elevator I looked over my shoulder. He was still standing there staring at me.

"Here's your coffee, Christina," I announced, poking my head through her door again.

She looked at me with her eyebrows bunched together. "Let me go ahead and clear my calendar." I outstretched the cup for her to take. "Definitely need to know what the cause of *that smile* is." She winked and I walked away.

The smile remained most of the day. The feeling it inspired I committed to memory. I could only consider it joy and wondered if I'd ever felt it before. It was new to me. I'd never experienced a calm, comforting peace like I did that day.

I credited God, and the long talks I'd been having with Him since the breakup. The talks where I pleaded for His forgiveness—for turning my back on Him. I asked for continued protection—of my heart and my body from any other person who wished to bring me harm. I thanked Him for His grace and mercy—that reminded me, despite anything I did, He still loved me.

Because after it was all said and done, Elijah hurt me. He broke me down and stomped on my ability to trust. But God could restore everything Elijah stole from me.

The joy I felt that day, was evidence of Him doing just what He had promised.

Chapter Ten

CODY

Hearing, "I'd like to go out with you," felt like every molecule in my body aligned at the same time and conspired to explode into little pieces. My entire being was bubbling with excitement, and still, I wanted to act as if I'd been on a date before. Like she wasn't the first person who ever accepted my offer.

But I couldn't convince my body to chill out.

Much like what was happening as I stood in front of her door. Staring at the wreath that hung beautifully, while flowers dangled in my hand at my side. Along with the molecules bubbling, my stomach was doing a dance of its own. Like it was auditioning for the ballet I was taking her to watch.

The smile on my face as I waited for her to open the door felt like it'd crack into two. Both sides of my mouth detaching from my face as it did.

Then the door opened, and the sight of her calmed every nerve that was firing, sat the ballerinas in my stomach aside, and eased my thumping heart.

"Morgan," I said softly as I lifted the flowers in front of me. "These are for you." As she took them I realized the other tragedy going on in my body—sweaty palms. I quickly wiped those down the sides of my jeans as she took the flowers and turned.

"Thank you," she said over her shoulder as she moved further into the house. "C'mon in," she laughed, "I'll get these in a vase then we can leave." I stepped through the threshold of her house but didn't advance further down the hallway. Instead, I watched as she gracefully walked away from me. The sway of her hips inviting my eyes into a trance I couldn't resist. "Gorgeous," I whispered, and it wasn't meant for her to hear it, but the moment it left my lips she turned over her shoulder again.

"What was that?" She tilted her head to the side, and her curls flopped into her face.

"I was just saying how gorgeous you are." The smile on her face danced again, and when it didn't disappear my body was set on fire. I heard a little giggle before the sound of a stream of water replaced it.

She emerged from the kitchen, and her descent toward me was even better than her retreat away from me. As badly as I wanted to look away, I couldn't. I stared at her until she met me, in front of the door. "I'm ready, if you are."

I ushered us from her front door. Hovering as she locked it, then held out my arm for her to take as we transcended down the stairs to my car. I was excited about the night I had planned, and as she asked where we were headed I was determined to keep it a surprise.

"I'm not sure I'm a fan of surprises," she told me as I navigated her neighborhood.

I laughed and asked, "And why is that?" Thinking of the many ways I'd love to surprise her in the future. It wasn't a thing for me in the past, but planning our date brought out a hint of excitement I didn't expect. Although, that could have been entirely because it was *her*.

"Because I don't know what I should expect."

"Isn't that the element of surprise?" I crooked my head her way.

"I should say, I've never been surprised before." I considered the years I knew she spent with Elijah and although we hadn't discussed them, or her current relationship status, I couldn't imagine a space where she wasn't fully appreciated. Where the person in her life wasn't doing everything in their power to make her happy, including a surprise or two.

"That's unfortunate. But be prepared to witness the sheer excitement of not knowing what to expect, and being thoroughly elated by whatever it is that awaits you on the other side of it."

"When you put it like that..." We both laughed.

We had a short drive to the theater, and I didn't want her mind spiraling in silence, so I asked, "How has your day been so far?"

"Honestly?" she asked with a solemn look on her face, and I nodded cautiously. "I've been torn."

"Torn?" Wasn't exactly the way I would have described my day leading up to the date. I was excited, nervous, eager. *But torn?*

"This is my first date with someone new in..." she sighed, "a really long time. And..." I probably shouldn't have been as excited as I was to learn that I was her first date in a while.

After all, I could have been her entry point only for her to launch into the dating game with *someone else*. "...I'm a little nervous." But the way her words trailed made me think there was something else left unsaid.

"But torn?" I iterated.

"I didn't expect that I'd be doing this again." Her head was facing toward the window, but I could hear the hurt in her voice and could only imagine the look that accompanied it.

I slid my hand across the console and rested it on her knee. "You don't have to tell me more than you are ready to share. And I hope tonight will ease your mind if nothing else."

She turned my direction and a little smile crept up on her face. I would have loved to see the huge grin, the sight of her when she giggled, or her shoulders relax, but I accepted everything she had to give.

"The theater?" She looked from the building to me as I pulled into a parking spot.

"Surprised?"

She laughed. "Actually, pleasantly." Then as I opened her car door she went on to tell me, "I heard the performance is amazing and wanted to check it out but didn't make time for it."

"And look at that, here we are."

I reached my hand out for her to take and was surprised myself when her delicate fingers interlaced with mine. We navigated to the door, through the atrium, and to our floor seats, before she dropped my hand. When she did, my hand felt cold.

She leaned over with the program propped up and began to describe what would unfold on stage. The gleam in her eyes noticeable even in the dim theater. "And this dancer here," she pointed to the book in her hands, "I hear she has a chance to join Alvin Ailey in New York." She might as well have been speaking Greek, but I didn't tell her those words didn't mean as much to me as they obviously did to her. Instead, I listened as she described what was clearly her passion until the lights dimmed further, and she eased back into her seat.

The dancers were moving effortlessly with grace across the stage, and for a moment I was captivated by their movement. Then I turned to the side and witnessed something even more fascinating than the dancers. Morgan's body had transformed. Her shoulders relaxed, an easy smile on her face, and wonder in her eyes as she followed the choreography of the ballerinas on stage.

More than the show, I wanted to watch her. I wondered what she would look like performing, and if she was still into it like she was in college. If somewhere in the city was a studio that had the privilege to see her body move like the dancers on stage.

As her mouth opened slightly, I forced myself to turn to the stage and watch the dancers gliding through the air. As beautiful as it was, it still didn't beat what I had sitting beside me.

She turned to me, and with my eyes steady on hers, she tilted her head and snickered. "Are you watching?"

"It's beautiful, right?" was all I could say in response.

Her gaze didn't stay on mine long. Her focus was on the performance. But mine stayed on her. Watching her as the show changed her expressions—so many emotions flashed across her face. Her body responding with each one. Sitting up as her face showed awe, and crouching back as she looked solemnly, the music along with each piece corresponding to the emotion she was expressing. Watching her was like a performance in itself, and when it was time for the interlude I was disappointed in the pause.

"I'm really enjoying myself, thank you for this."

Nodding, I asked her, "Do you still dance?"

Then as if the keys of the piano were slowing, and a daunting tale was being told in the melody, her face turned downward. "Not anymore."

Like hers did during the show, my face transformed into a solemn stare. "Why is that?"

"I think," she said, pulling her purse into her hand, "I should use the restroom before the show starts back up."

I nodded, "Of course," as I stood, allowing her to slide past me.

When she returned, the lights were dimming again, and she settled into her seat without a word to me. For the second half of the show I committed myself to watching the performance, if for nothing other than to have something to discuss with her afterward. I didn't want her to think I wasn't interested in the performance, because I was, especially seeing how much she was intrigued by it.

As the show ended, and the curtains closed, I was relieved that I could turn my attention back to her.

Outside in the cooler air, I asked, "Are you hungry?"

She nodded slightly. "Maybe something light."

As I drove through the city in search of a restaurant, the car was overtaken by silence despite my attempts to ask her about the performance. Her responses weren't non-existent, just short, quick, and I missed what we were forming before the show.

When I opened her car door and attempted to reach for

her hand, it went to her sweater, tugging it tight around her chest. I wanted to ask her what happened from the interlude—when everything shifted—but decided not to.

Seated across from each other, I quickly found something I wanted to eat and turned my attention to her. But her gaze stayed on the menu until the waiter arrived.

Then finally, she asked, "Why'd you pick the ballet?"

I thought it was a given considering her love for the art, but I explained, "I know you used to love the ballet and thought you'd enjoy it."

She nodded, "I used to," with a somber look on her face. "But why go through all this trouble when you could have done something simple like take me out to dinner and drinks?"

"Simple?" I laughed. "I don't think there's anything simple about you. And you deserve better than basic."

Her eyes widened at my response, but it wasn't meant to surprise her. It was the truth.

"Why me?" I could have told her obviously, why not her, but I felt like she needed more than that. Whatever it was that had her doubting that she deserved to be treated better than basic, could have been the same thing that dimmed her light. The thing that was making her far less vibrant than she was in college. Or I could have told her how I would have loved to have the opportunity to take her out in college. How I would have loved to get to know more about her back then. Like outside of ballet, what did she love? I could have told her that despite the years that passed since then, nothing about the desire to get to know her had changed.

But I felt she needed something else. Because she needed to know, despite what I wanted or desired, that she deserved the best. So, I settled with, "You are amazing. Kind, gentle, sexy." I stopped there and hoped that would bring a smile to her face, then I continued when a little one snuck out. "Your laughter is contagious, and on top of all that you are accomplished." She cleared her throat and looked away from me. I went on to say, "That day a couple of months ago in the café, I couldn't have been more excited to see a familiar face, but there was something about you that day that wasn't like it was ten years ago."

She looked down at the table.

I reached across and touched the top of her hand softly until she looked at me again. "I don't know what God has planned for me, or you. Or us." I held that thought for a minute. "Whatever it is, if I find that the only purpose I'm serving right now is to restore whatever it was that you lost, I'll feel accomplished."

A single tear slid down her cheek and I reached over and flicked it away. "Please don't cry." I felt the tug in my own chest as I watched her try to compose herself.

She dabbed her napkin to her eyes then said, "I wasn't expecting such a thoughtful response."

Chapter Eleven

MORGAN

In all the years I spent with Elijah he knew my love of ballet intimately. When we first started dating, I'd have to rush our time together so that I wouldn't be late for a dance class. Or sometimes I'd be too busy preparing for a performance we hardly had time to see each other. Despite that, if I asked him to join me at a ballet performance, he'd easily decline.

He only attended my performances because I'd beg him for weeks before, and even then, I found he'd leave before the performance was over. When other performers had their boyfriends and family gathering around, showering them with love and flowers, I'd scan the crowd in hopes he'd be there. And he wasn't.

It was something I learned to get over. I found other people to watch my performances, until I finally stopped performing. Then after college, when I started working, it was easy to stop dancing altogether. Not having the support from him made all the difference for me.

As I sat across from Cody, after sitting beside him at the ballet performance, I had more than a few emotions surging through my body. I probably would have fared better if he would have taken me to a bowling alley.

But crying, on a date, was the last thing I wanted to be doing.

The pleas from my mind to the corners of my eyes were going unanswered, and the tears shed. Explaining everything that was behind the tears would have caused more, so I avoided it.

"What is it you like to do in your free time?" I asked, hoping a change of subject would get my emotions in check, at least until we were out of the restaurant. I tried remembering back to school and told him, "In college, seems you were very much into computers."

His face contorted before he explained, "I definitely was, but now I prefer interacting with people in real life." He smiled. "I like the arts—museums, art exhibits, concerts, live poetry." My heart was fluttering as he described the different arts.

"Really?" I quizzed him, "What was the last exhibit you visited?"

"There was one," he started, and by the way his face lit up I could tell it must have been impactful, "before I left California, it was an ode to Black culture." I narrowed my eyes. "It was different, but I really enjoyed it."

"You're very surprising," I finally told him.

"Here we are." The server stood beside our table placing our plates in front of us, but my eyes remained on Cody.

Love is Patient

"How so?" He tilted his head to the side after the server walked away.

I considered how he was different from Elijah, drastically so. "Just something about you seems unapologetically you. And with it you seem just genuinely in a good space."

He shook his head and told me, "It took some time to get here, but thank you for recognizing it."

I wanted to know more about that, the Cody before the man that sat in front of me. "Care to elaborate?" I was interested in knowing more about him and felt like it was a good way to distract him from me.

"In school, I quickly became obsessed with technology and solutions." He admitted, "I let personal relationships falter." He winced. "You know I never dated anyone in college?"

I wagged my head and told him, "I know a few guys who didn't date but did other things."

He smiled and said, "Didn't do much of those *other things* either."

"Oh."

"Right. I stopped going to church." That statement more than the others made my stomach tie into knots. Elijah wasn't a churchgoer and it was another thing that became a sticking point in our relationship.

"And now?"

"Me and God are good. I try to be in somebody's service every Sunday. Now that I'm back here, I need to find a church I can attend regularly." Then he asked, "Any recommendations?"

I panicked. I hadn't returned to church yet. Had long stopped going to church every Sunday. And didn't dare tell him I had just started praying again. "I don't, but if you find one, maybe you can let me know."

His eyebrows stitched together, and he asked, "But you do believe, right?"

I could sense the hesitation in his voice as he asked, almost as if he didn't truly want to know the answer. I knew that feeling. Knowing that the person you spent time with didn't believe. Reconciling those thoughts was always a challenge for me.

Emphatically, I nodded. "I do." And thankfully, that was what never changed. No matter what Elijah stole from me, he didn't take my belief away. Although he hedged a fence around it, it remained intact. "Right now," I looked up into his eyes and hoped he believed me when I said, "I'm fixing what had been broken."

He nodded. "Understandable. If you are working on it, I'm sure God will meet you in the middle."

I smiled. "I'm going to stand on that."

His plate was empty, and I had hardly touched the shrimp skewers on mine. "I was going to ask if you wanted dessert, but…" I followed his eyes down to my plate and scrunched my nose.

"I think I'll just box this up. I'm sure I'll get hungry later," I told him.

"Sure." He asked the server for a box, and I watched his interaction with the guy. It was kind, and I realized that's just who he was. A nice guy. And I wasn't used to the nice guys. Didn't see them around my mama, and even the ones who had ever approached me I overlooked them.

As much as I wanted to see what it'd be like to be with a nice guy, I didn't want my mess to ruin him.

When he pulled in front of my house, he turned off the

Love is Patient

car and was prepared to step out, but I stopped him. "Cody," I said softly, "I need to tell you something." He sat back in his seat and his eyes were focused on me. "I don't think it would be fair to you if I rushed into anything right now."

He wiped a hand across his beard but didn't respond.

"I think I have some things I need to work out first. Definitely some things I need to get over."

As I sat there with my chest heaving, I felt his hand covering mine. "Like I said before, even if I'm only here to help you get over it, I'm good with that." He smiled slightly and I felt my body relax. "I'm here for whatever you need."

My body started to warm in response to his offer, and I knew I needed to get into the house before I did something I'd regret. "Thank you," I whispered and looked up to the house.

He still opened my car door, offered me his arm, and walked me up the steps. He lingered as I opened the door, and when I was finally inside, he told me, "Thank you for tonight."

I smirked. "No, honestly, thank you."

We stood in the doorway awkwardly before I leaned forward and wrapped my arms around him and rested my head on his chest. As soon as I felt his arms around my waist, there was a warmth that cradled me and I didn't want to let go.

But he tugged away first, telling me, "Have a good night, Morgan," before he walked away. I closed the door behind me and stood there listening to his footsteps as they hit the concrete. When I heard the roar of his car engine I let my head rest against the door.

With tears streaming down my face, and my eyes clutched closed, I started praying, "Dear God, Cody is an amazing man. I hope his intentions are pure, and he won't turn out like Elijah. I know my heart isn't ready right now to be opened back up, and as I prepare myself for that I don't want to hurt Cody in the process. Please God, protect him, as you restore me." I sniffled and took a deep breath in before reciting, "Amen."

Chapter Twelve

CODY

Not a single day went by that I wasn't checking in on Morgan. Sometimes it was as soon as I woke up, sending her a text to simply say, "I hope you have a good day." Or in between classes to ask, "How's your day so far?" Other times, late at night as I eased myself into bed, and just before I shut my eyes, I'd say, "Hope you had a good day, and sleep well."

She'd respond, sometimes with similar words, and sometimes with a little less. Just telling me she had a good day, or telling me, "Goodnight."

I was content with those messages, and the idea I hadn't had the privilege of running into her around the city. I had to resist the urge to ask her out again, especially after she told me she needed to pump the brakes on dating.

I knew she had some things to work out, and I supported that whole-heartedly. The passing time wasn't excruciating, and I genuinely hoped she would get back to where she was before whatever it was that destroyed her.

I could have occupied my time with the random women who were finding their way into my office on campus, or the ladies I'd meet during the welcome at church. I wasn't intrigued by Matthew's offers to join him in Raleigh for happy hour either. There was only one woman I was interested in pursuing, and if time was what she needed before I could fully engage with her, time was what I was going to give her.

But when the response to my afternoon text message asking how her day was going wasn't answered with a simple reply, I pushed my need to give her space aside. Seeing "I'm having a rough day" led me to send her a different type of text.

Cody: Come to my house.

The thought sprung from my fingers before I could fully consider what I was typing. *What could I do to help with her feelings?*

I had some time to think about that because her response didn't come back quickly, and I even thought it wouldn't come at all. I had made it home and started thinking about what I was going to eat for dinner before I heard my phone vibrate with a message.

Morgan: What's your address?

Quickly, I typed it out and she told me she'd be there soon. I looked around my apartment and when I settled on the fact it was in decent shape, I pulled a blanket from the closet and placed it on the couch. Then I went to my kitchen, pulled a mug from the cabinet and tea from the drawer, and started heating a kettle full of water.

By the time I heard the knock at the door, I had a cup of tea ready for her. "Come on in," I said as I opened the door. If I would have seen Morgan before she told me she had a rough day, I would have been able to guess it.

The makeup on her face was smeared, her curls were pulled into a messy ponytail, and there was a frown that looked like it was overpowering her ability to smile. Even a little bit.

"I'm not sure why I showed up," she said, walking behind me. "I should have gone home and climbed into the bed."

I didn't respond until we were in front of the couch. "Here," I told her, "Make yourself comfortable." She hesitated at first. "You know," I pulled her purse from her shoulder, "sit." And as she did, I looked up at her before removing her shoes. "And relax." Then I grabbed the blanket I had waiting on her and placed it over her lap.

The frown she was wearing was replaced with narrowed eyes as she looked at me suspiciously. I left her wondering as I went into the kitchen and grabbed the warm cup of tea. "I hope you drink tea." I assured her, "It's chamomile so it should help you relax."

She took it in her hands and after blowing it then taking a sip, she said, "This is a pleasant surprise." But the words were strained, as if she didn't believe them herself.

I sat beside her and said, "I tried to tell you about surprises." I smiled.

She laughed and said, "You nurturing me is not anything I would have ever imagined."

Her hand circled around the mug as she stared into the

darkened water. "You know," her eyes looked up to mine, "I don't think it's anything I would have done for anyone else. But—"

"You pity me?" Her voice was strained as she said it.

"Not at all. Just felt like something that would be helpful." I second-guessed myself before telling her, "If it's too much," I reached for the mug and she shook her head with a gentle smile. "No?"

"No."

We sat quietly as she sipped the tea, and as her sips slowed, I put an arm around her shoulder and said, "Feel like talking about it?" as I eased her closer to me.

"I can usually manage the day on little sleep." My jaw tensed at the revelation that she hadn't been sleeping. "Today, there was a lot going on in the office, and I felt like I couldn't keep up." Her voice started to quiver. "And I found myself getting angry. Angry that I hadn't been sleeping." She paused. "Then angry that I couldn't keep up." She huffed. "It was a mess."

I felt her shoulders shudder, and I held her a little tighter before asking, "You haven't been sleeping?"

Her head shook against my arm.

Since she didn't elaborate, I asked, "Why not?"

With a mocking laugh, she said, "Guess after years of sleeping next to someone I have a hard time falling asleep." Then she declared, "By the time I doze off I'm awakened by the alarm clock." She joked, "It's torture."

"I bet." Then I made myself comfortable on the couch, placing my feet on the coffee table, and told her, "Consider me your pillow."

She adjusted out of my arms until her face met mine. "You sure about that?" I nodded and rested my head back on the couch. There were worse ways I could have spent my evening than being cuddled up with her in my arms.

She placed the mug on the table beside my feet then stretched her body along the couch, and finally rested her head on my chest. I slid my hand against her arm until I heard soft snores that turned into louder ones.

Watching her sleep, I prayed, "God, whatever it is that is troubling her, lighten her load. Bless her with peace, and if she must endure this burden for what you have in store for her, let her trust I'm here to help her carry it. Amen."

I shifted from under her and placed a pillow under her head. She adjusted, her snoring paused for a minute before she was fast asleep again.

I made my way to the kitchen and finished looking through my fridge for dinner. What would have been dinner for one, became dinner for two, just in case she was hungry when she woke up.

Grabbing the ingredients, I tried to make as little noise as possible as I moved around the kitchen. Slicing the vegetables took a little longer, as I wasn't chopping like the people in an industrial kitchen. I placed pots on the stove and stood close by as the meal started to form—smothered steak, potatoes, and green peas. The scent had my stomach growling and I was ready to dig in, okay with the fact that Morgan was still stretched out on my couch.

But just as I pulled a plate from the cabinet, I saw her head pop up over the couch. She looked around before her eyes settled on me, and I asked, "Hungry?"

"Actually," she nodded, "I am. But—"

"Then come eat." Her eyes were questioning, and I assured her, "Trust me, I cooked enough for both of us." I looked at the pots and said, "Maybe even a few more," with a laugh.

"Mind if I use your restroom first?" I directed her to the door down the hall and when she returned, she told me, "I can't believe I showed up to your house looking like a whole entire mess." Her eyes were wide as she joined me near the stove. "What'd you cook?" she asked, peering over my shoulder.

I was piling our plates as I answered, "Smothered steak, potatoes, and green peas."

"Spoken like a true country boy."

"You can take the boy out the country, but not the country out the boy." I winked and I saw her cheeks flush. "Sit down, I'll serve you."

"You sir, are too kind." But her words again were strained as she said it.

"From the sound of it, I don't know if that's a good thing or a bad thing." I placed a plate in front of her as I went to collect mine and join her at the table.

"I don't think it's bad." Her hand reached across the table and rested in mine before I offered to say grace. "Mind if I say it?" I shook my head. "God, we thank you for this food, and I thank you for allowing Cody to prepare it. For his welcoming heart to let me in, even as I am," her hand tightened around mine before she whispered, "Amen."

"Amen." I wanted to ask about the man who was occupying her bed, who left her alone and unable to sleep. But decided it wasn't the best line of questioning after she just woke from a nap and looked much more rested than when she arrived. "How does it taste?"

Her mouth formed around her fork, and I watched in

anticipation for her response but got lost on her lips and the way she licked them after finishing the bite. "Not bad at all."

I wagged my head. "I'll take it," I told her, "My mama doesn't cook as much as she used to so sometimes I try to replicate her recipes." I laughed. "But have you ever had a Black woman tell you a recipe?" Morgan snickered. "Lots of season with love and until you feel it's enough. Every meal is dependent on how I feel that day," I rambled on, "And it never seems to be the same from day to day."

She laughed, and once she started she couldn't stop. Her hand flew to her mouth as she tried to conceal the loud-pitched sound, but I reached across the table and told her, "Oh no, I want to hear all of that."

Then she stopped abruptly, her lip tugging between her teeth. "I don't know why I could imagine your mama telling you that." She started again, and this time I joined her.

"Maybe you can meet her one day. She's great."

"If the way she raised you is any indication, I bet she is."

With my hand over my chest, I told her, "She'd be happy to hear that."

Since moving back to North Carolina, I saw my mama a handful of times, but even that was better than how many times I saw her when I lived in California. Although she joked that I should be starting a life of my own, I knew she enjoyed my visits as much as I did. I couldn't imagine having anything less than that with my mama. Looking at Morgan, I asked, "What about your family?" It wasn't something I remember ever talking about when we were in school. If our conversations weren't about our classwork, she'd manage to slip in something about dance, and eventually Elijah too, but never her family.

"My sister, Mia, lives in Texas." Her face was bright as

she described her little sister. "Wish we could see each other more often." Then she looked at me skeptically and said, "Guess there is one good thing out of technology we can grasp onto. Those video calls make a world of difference."

I had to agree, "You're right, they do." But I wasn't in the classroom, so I didn't feel the need to tell her that video calls also distracted people from everyday interactions. The reliance on a video call to supplement in-person visits was detrimental to relationships, at times. "And your parents?"

"Well," she declared, "I've never known my father." Before I could comment she said, "And my mom, she's in Florida." Her lips curled up as if she wasn't excited about that detail.

"Do you see her often?"

She twisted her lips before replying, "Not as often as I should." Then she added, "Especially since she doesn't ever leave Florida."

The way she explained their relationship had me thinking I needed to call my parents and thank them for being supportive. I was only in California for a couple of years, but they loved to hop on a flight to visit me.

After a long sigh and a distant stare, Morgan said, "I can help clean." She stood from the table and insisted, "It's the least I can do."

Only because I didn't want our time to end did I accept her offer. "I'll wash, you dry?" She nodded and listened as I told her where to place different dishes. When we were finished she said she should be leaving.

"After that meal, the tea, and the little nap, I might actually be relaxed enough to sleep well tonight." She nudged me in the side. "I feel bad that you did all that and I can't offer you anything in return that would benefit you."

Love is Patient

I toyed with the words in my mind before replying, "Life isn't always about what you can receive, sometimes there is joy in giving." I stretched my arms open, and she walked into them. Like the first time we hugged, there was a warmth I couldn't explain with her head on my chest and her arms around my waist. It felt like my mama's apple pie, it just felt like *home*.

And when she walked out of my arms, I imagined my mama swatting my hand, telling me I had to save some for later, as she asked, "Do you remember Elijah?"

Ice water splashed in my face would have been better than hearing her whisper his name softly. I would have preferred walking barefoot across broken glass than to hear the pain as she continued, "He went to A&T, and he was my boyfriend freshman year."

I wanted, more than anything, for her to stop describing him. So quickly, I answered, "Yes, I remember him." She leaned against my kitchen counter and plucked at her fingernails.

"I'm not sure if you knew this or not, but we dated throughout college." She paused and looked at me, so I nodded, hoping we could skip the details of their relationship. Still wondering how in that moment he was on her mind. "Dated even after," she hurried with the next part, "I don't think in all the years we were together he ever did anything with the understanding it was just to make me happy."

A lump grew in my throat, and I wanted to pull her back into my arms, erase every thought of Elijah and what he did, or didn't, with her.

"I hate that for you. I hate that he didn't fully appreciate you."

Her eyes met mine and I assumed I'd see a tear when she

said, "That day you saw me in the café," I stared at her, waiting for her to elaborate, "the first day of school." Her breathing became heavier. "We had just broken up the night before."

The sight of her—how deflated she looked—made sense. "God's timing is impeccable." I knew if I would have seen her before then it would have been much like it was in college when I wanted to so badly ask her out but could only see the love she had for Elijah in her eyes when she looked at me.

"It seems it is," she whispered. "Alright, I better let you get to your evening. I've taken up enough of your time."

I wanted to scream, "Stay," because I could have spent every minute of the rest of that night talking to her. She had already moved into the living room and slid into her shoes, pulled her purse on her shoulder, and was headed to the front door though.

"Just know, if you ever need a human pillow again, I got you."

She nodded. "Thank you." She reached her hand out to my arm and I felt the delicate caress of her fingers, and then she was gone. I watched her walk down the hallway until I couldn't see her anymore.

Chapter Thirteen

MORGAN

Ava heard half the story of Cody nurturing me at his house and blurted, "You need to cook for that man." As if my cooking was some award-winning, must-try experience.

It was not.

Even still, I agreed. I felt after everything he did for me that night, I wanted to give him some of what he had poured into me. I just didn't think the simple act of cooking for another man would be laced with the level of anxiety I had as I moved through my kitchen.

It wasn't that I wasn't a decent cook, and I didn't have a recipe on deck with all the suggested ingredients. Because I did. The meal was even one I had cooked before and loved.

It was the memory of cooking for Elijah that had me panicking. Ava was on the phone telling me, "Morgan, it's going to be fine. Cody has already proved a hundred times over that he is nothing like Elijah."

"But even Elijah in the beginning was nothing like Elijah in the end."

"Facts." She hesitated, likely struggling with words that could console me in my fury of trying to coax myself into an excuse for canceling with Cody.

"I should just call him and cancel."

"Or not. You will not do that." Her response was firm, definitive, as if she had any control over what I would do after we were off the phone with each other. "Morgan, you've already told him you need to take it slow. And this time around you know what signs to look for. You know how to avoid a no-good, terrible, bad-for-you relationship."

I laughed. "Guess it was that bad, huh?"

"And was." Then what she said next made me realize just how bad it was. "I would have told you sophomore year, that time when he yelled at you for being a few minutes late to his dorm." Then she added, "Or that time when he threw your book to the ground after he told you he was going to drop out, as if it was your fault he had the bright idea to leave school and chase his dreams."

I leaned against the counter, tears threatening to fall when I told her, "Promise me, if you see any red flags I ignore, now and till forever, tell me."

"And you promise me you won't get upset if I have to tell you."

"Promise," we both repeated.

Then I heard my doorbell and froze. "If that's him," I said with a shaky voice, "he's early." I looked around the kitchen at the scattered ingredients.

"Guess he can help," she offered, as if it was a simple solution to a complicated problem.

"Let me get the door," I told her, "I'll call you later." I

wiped my hands across a towel and walked slowly down the hallway.

A bouquet of flowers was outstretched and blocking the person holding them. As beautiful as they were, I don't think it compared to the smile he was rocking when I took them. "I hope you don't mind that I'm early. I was kinda just sitting around the house and thought I could be of help to you."

I laughed. "Of help, to me?" Then I told him, "You aren't supposed to show up on a date and help."

"Oh, so this is a date?" His question caught me off guard, and I looked over my shoulder with wide eyes as I walked toward the kitchen. "I was just thinking it was the two of us getting together to eat." He winked. "You know, for the person who isn't really ready to *date* yet."

I smiled. "Right, just two people having a meal together."

If that's what it was, my body didn't get the memo. My heart started racing when the word "date" was uttered.

"How about you just keep me company," I said as I tried to gather my thoughts in the kitchen.

"If that's what you want, I can do that," he said, removing his coat and taking a seat at the counter. "What are you cooking anyway?"

I was walking the cutting board to the stove when the sound of his voice made my hands shake, and half the vegetables went crashing onto the floor. He hopped up from his seat, grabbed a napkin, and helped me clean it up. "Sure you don't want any help? I can cut up more vegetables if you'd like."

"No," I sighed, "It's okay. I'll take care of it." I shook my hands at my side and attempted the task again, making sure I moved a little slower.

"Do you cook often?"

"It probably doesn't look like it." I laughed. "Not with my extreme anxiety over here dropping vegetables, and nowhere near finished with the meal." He shrugged. "It's another casualty of my relationship. I cooked often, but…" I didn't know how to describe what happened with us when I did cook. "Often he wouldn't join me, or he'd criticize what I cooked." Then I thought that made it sound like my food was about to be disgusting, so I retorted, "I can cook though."

But as I turned over my shoulder, I saw him standing closely behind me. "You don't have to worry about either of those situations tonight. I'll eat whatever you grace my plate with." Then he pointed, "And I'll be sitting right there across from you." He rubbed his hands down the sides of my arms. "But none of that can happen if you burn up the food. So let me know how I can help."

I laughed. "Okay," I told him, "Watch the rice for me to make sure it doesn't stick." He nodded. "And I'll work on the stir-fry."

"Sounds like a plan to me." As he leaned against the counter, in view of the pot of rice, he asked, "Did you sleep okay last night?"

"Not nearly as good as I did when I napped at your house, but it wasn't as bad as it's been."

He tilted his head as he stuck a spoon into the rice and stirred. "Told you, a full-size, self-heating human body pillow right here." He tapped his chest and smiled. I felt my body warming at the thought of laying my head on his chest again, of being so close to him I could hear his heart beating.

I focused my attention on the vegetables in the pot I was stirring, and not on thoughts of his body entangled with mine. "I think this is finished," I told him as I looked over the beef to make sure it was cooked thoroughly. "Ready to eat?"

He closed his eyes and sniffed the air in front of the stove. "It smells appetizing. I can't wait to dig in." I avoided staring at him because I just knew one look at his mouth after those words left it may have found us in a place I wasn't ready to go yet.

I cleared my throat and told him, "Let me just grab the plates," as I brushed past him.

We sat across from each other, bowed our heads, and he said grace. The gesture was starting to feel natural, so much so, I'd remembered to say grace myself *before* taking the first bite, even when I was eating alone.

He didn't speak after his first bite, not even the second or third, and I was worried that he didn't like the food. Finally, I asked, "Does it taste okay?"

With his fork mid-air, he looked at me and apologized, "Sorry about that, I don't think I was expecting it to taste this good."

I huffed, "So, you were expecting me not to be able to cook?"

He shook his head. "Not at all, but there's like cooking to survive, then there's cooking and making it something I'd want to live off of."

My eyes widened and again, I felt my cheeks warming. "Wow." He was back to eating before he asked what I had planned for Thanksgiving. "I forgot it was coming up."

"Forgot?" He laughed. "As much as I like to eat, it's the one holiday I prepare for in advance."

Laughing, I asked, "And how does one prepare for Thanksgiving?"

"Well, you start with eating lots of small meals throughout the day a week leading up to the big meal. Then," in all seriousness, he told me, "the day of, you are ready to eat as much as you want. Multiple plates, you know?" He shrugged his shoulders. "Are you cooking?"

I shook my head. I had never cooked a Thanksgiving meal. At the most, we'd visit Elijah's parents' house and by the time we arrived the food was already done.

"Are you?"

The look of disgust on his face made my own contort. "I'll be at my parents' house. So..." He put his fork down for the first time since he started eating. "Are you headed to Florida to spend the holidays with your mom?"

"Her house is the last place I want to be for the holidays." I could have easily gotten on a flight to visit her, but as I told him, "I don't think I should be around her right now." He looked at me with his eyes narrowed and I explained, "After my breakup, I don't think I need to be around her and whatever guy is taking up her space. It'll just be too much of a reminder of how things ended."

"I'm not sure I understand." I had already said too much and leaving him hanging felt unfair.

I grabbed my drink and sipped before telling him, "Ever since I can remember, my mom's been in an abusive relationship."

His eyes widened and he sat back in his seat. "I'm sorry to hear that." Then his eyes darkened, similar to how Elijah's darkened that night we fought. Although, an immediate flush of my body or quivering hands didn't come. I didn't fear anything Cody would do next. But I wasn't ready to explain the response needed to answer his question. "Morgan," his voice was measured, gentle, "Did Elijah hit you?" His head was tilted to the side, his hands clutched in front of him as he leaned forward.

Quickly, I told him, "Nothing like my mom's been

through. It was only once." I was proud to tell him, "Thank God, once was all it took for me to leave him." I clarified, "I know for many women that's not the case. It isn't easy to make that decision." His slow blinks, his silence, the way he just sat stone faced across from me was alarming. "Are you okay?"

He bit his lip, and finally his head hung. After he wiped a hand across his face, his eyes met mine and he explained, "Once is too many times. There's never a reason for a man to put his hands on a woman." He growled, "Never."

I wondered if he felt the same about a man putting his hands on another, because the look in his eyes had me worried for the off chance he ever encountered Elijah in person.

"You're right. Once is one time too many." My hand instinctively went to the areas on my arm that were bruised from Elijah's grip. And the soreness in my cheek, that had long gone way, seemed to be throbbing again. I knew that if just talking about it with Cody was enough to elicit that type of response from my body, seeing a man get remotely close to my mom would cause me to do something I wasn't prepared to defend.

"Another meal ruined by Elijah," I said with sarcasm, "And he isn't even here." My fork hovered over my plate as I questioned my appetite after only finishing a few bites.

"There are clearly some landmines I know better to avoid now." I watched as he stood from his seat and walked to my side of the table. "But the last thing I'm willing to do is to let him, and your past, haunt you." With his hand in mine, he tugged me up from my seat, edged my chin up, then wrapped his arms around my waist. "I know it will be difficult for you to move on, to forget, just know I'm willing to help you overcome it."

That sound of fireworks exploding at the end of the Fourth of July. When the person lighting them goes crazy, lighting multiple fireworks at a time. That's what it felt like inside my chest. Every firework I had on reserve was lit, all at once, by Cody.

Then amidst the firework show happening inside, I felt his warm lips on my forehead, and I could hardly contain my emotions. I was tired of crying though, especially over things that should have been joyful moments. So, I sucked it up, fought the tears back, and leaned my head up until I saw his face. "I like the sound of that."

"How do you like the sound of joining me for Thanksgiving at my parents' house?" The look in his eyes was promising, the darkened orbs were no longer there, and a small smile waited on his face.

The little I knew about his family wasn't enough for me to make a complete judgment on them, but if they were anything like him, I knew I would feel welcomed. "It's the first one I've been to in a while since I tried to make it home for Christmas when I was on the West Coast. Doing both was a little challenging," he explained.

"Your first one in a while, and I'd be with you?" He shrugged like he was asking me to ride with him to the gas station. I laughed. "That doesn't seem like a big deal to you?"

He leaned against the table and moved me between his legs. "Are you thinking you coming home with me would imply we were a couple?" His eyes were narrowing like it was an honest question, but I couldn't imagine a time when that's not exactly what everyone would think.

"That's what I'd think if it was my sister bringing a guy home."

He reached for my hand and held it between both of his. "I'll let them know we are just friends."

Although that's what I wanted, to take things slow, to not rush into something my heart wasn't ready for, hearing him say "just friends" felt like a dagger through the heart, twisted and turned just enough to remind me it was piercing the middle of my chest.

He eyed me cautiously until I replied, "Thanksgiving, with your family, just friends. Let's do it," I whispered finally.

Chapter Fourteen

CODY

An invite to Thanksgiving seemed innocent enough. Sure, I hadn't invited anyone home with me before. But hearing that Morgan didn't have plans made it an easy decision to ask her to join me. I didn't consider the implications to my family by asking her; it wasn't as important to me.

The hesitation from her, the way I held my breath every time we spoke thinking she'd change her mind, had thrown me for a loop that week. Finally, on Thanksgiving morning, as I walked the steps to her door, I anticipated the worst and was pleasantly surprised when she opened the door with a small smile on her face.

As we drove from Greensboro to Raleigh, I gave her details about my family. Telling her about my sister, "Although she's only two years older than me, nobody can tell her she isn't my mama."

The air that Morgan sucked at the sound of that made my head turn her way. "Protective?"

"Somewhat," I confirmed. "And my mom, she's easygoing but passionate." I could see Morgan's face growing weary, and I noted, "Okay, this isn't helping." Her fingers tapped a tune on her legs, and I just wanted to make sure she was comfortable. That her Thanksgiving wasn't a reminder of those from the past. "What'd you like to know about them?"

"Your family sounds very accomplished. What do they like to do for fun?"

I was proud to say, "Attend galas, they are really into the arts as well." Then I conceded, "At least my parents are. I have no idea what my sister does for fun. She's a traveling nurse and is always on the go."

"And she's single?"

"As far as I know." I shrugged. "As far as I know she isn't bringing anyone home with her." The words slipped from my mouth and as soon as I saw her sideways glance, I said, "I mean, don't worry." I fumbled over the next words, "I told them *we* are just friends."

She wore a smirk on her face until I pulled into the driveway of my parents' house, then she pulled her lip between her teeth and stared at the garage door.

I reached over the console and interlaced our fingers. "I promise, it'll be cool. We'll fill ourselves with good food, chat it up, then be headed back home in time for you to crawl into bed."

When she didn't release her lip, I pulled her wrist to my mouth and placed a gentle kiss there. "Tell me how I can make you comfortable."

Her eyes were connected with her wrist and didn't leave

the spot where the kiss landed. "Probably shouldn't do that," she said softly, and a small smile crept up her face. "You know, because we are just friends."

I heard "because we are just friends" and knew we were taking it slow, but I was confused at the sarcasm that aligned with it.

I tilted my head to the side and repeated it back to her, "just friends." Except, just friends would imply that my heart didn't skip a beat at the sound of every word that graced her lips. That my palms didn't sweat when she was around, or the urge to pull her close wasn't a constant thought on my mind whenever she was near. But if "just friends" was what we were calling what was transpiring between the two of us, I'd be "just friends" for an eternity.

Another glance at the house and she suggested, "Should we go inside?"

"We should." I was excited, not only to be home, but for the food that awaited us inside. I opened her car door and resisted the instinct to place a hand on her lower back, to wrap my fingers around hers, or inch my body nearby. I led the way as she walked slowly behind me.

The front door opened before I could even knock and my mom stood with outstretched arms. "You're here," she said with a warm smile. But as I tried to walk into her arms, she nudged me aside and looked at Morgan. "It's great to meet you. Come on in." I scoffed and my mama laughed. "How was the drive?"

"It wasn't too bad, Mrs. Felix." Morgan's voice was soft as she responded to all my mama's hundred questions.

"Well come on in here," she told her, "Food is almost ready, but you can join me and Natalie while Cody finds his daddy."

Love is Patient

Morgan shot me a knowing look over her shoulder and I wanted to intercede. "Mama—"

"She'll be fine, Cody. Promise."

They disappeared and I went to the living room where I heard the television up louder than necessary. "Hey Pops," I said to my dad, who was perched in front of the TV with a magazine on his lap.

"Cody," he looked beyond me, "Where's your *friend*?"

I smiled. "Mom took her into the kitchen." I sat at the edge of the couch. "Should I be worried?" His lips tightened and he stared into his magazine again. "Of course, I should," I huffed.

"Your mama is just excited you are back on the East Coast."

"Uh huh," I murmured as I watched the door and tried to listen for Morgan's voice over the TV speakers. "Why is this up so loud?" I said, searching for the remote.

"Sounds fine to me, son." I looked over at my dad who had a half-smile on his face. "Just sit back and relax. I'm sure the young woman you brought can manage herself just fine. Your mama doesn't bite, I promise."

"It's just that…" I started and stopped because I didn't know why I was so anxious about my mama having Morgan cornered in the kitchen. The two of us weren't hiding anything, and we were just friends as I told my parents. I just didn't want Morgan to feel any more uncomfortable than she already was for joining me.

"Oh, so this whole friend thing is a ruse?" My dad hadn't even looked up from his magazine as he said it. "It wasn't you who suggested the reference of the title?" I steepled my hands in my lap and shook my head, although he wasn't looking my direction. "That happens. But if she's here with you today, maybe something will eventually transpire." He reminded me, "Being a woman's friend is a way to prove to her that you'll have her best interest at heart. Rushing into a relationship would imply that it's your desires you are trying to meet." His eyes finally looked up and he said, "Patience is a virtue, son, and you'd be wise to practice it." Then he went on to say, "It's also a characteristic of love."

I turned my head to look at him, his eyes still in the magazine but a wide smile on his face. "Love?" I croaked. Years of the same woman on my mind could have been considered *strong feelings* for sure, but I hadn't upgraded it to love. It wasn't something I considered, and honestly, I wasn't rushing into satisfying my own desires with Morgan. I didn't explain it to my dad, but I knew ultimately, whatever happened, I wanted Morgan to trust again. To feel appreciated and cared for. Even if that meant we would remain friends.

"Son, it's written all over your face." It couldn't have been in that moment. Because in that moment, my nose was scrunched, my lips twisted, and my eyebrows bunched together. Wasn't exactly what I envisioned love would look like. Still, he wasn't even looking at me so he couldn't have perceived all that anyway.

I laughed. "Okay, Pops. If you say so."

His eyes rose to meet mine and he nodded subtly. "I do."

I tried for the next hour to focus my attention on the football game unfolding on the TV. To listen to the commentators as they detailed each play, and the referee calls, to laugh at the commercials.

I failed. As hard as I tried to hear the TV, I could only listen for the soft whispers of Morgan's voice in the distance. My sister's loud cackle and my mother's comforting voice were what overtook the noise in the living room.

Then, finally, I heard my sister's voice when she announced, "Time to eat." If I were an athlete, it would have been no surprise how quickly I leaped from the couch to my feet.

Even my dad noticed. "Excited to eat, son?" A little laugh as he walked ahead of me. "I get like that too. Your mama's sweet potato pie is something else." Then he looked behind him and said, "But I'm sure you are excited about something more than her pie this year, right?"

I put a hand to his shoulder and said, "Chill, Pops," with a chuckle as we made our way to the dining room where all the food was placed in the middle of the table.

"This smells amazing." I stood in between my mom and Morgan, ready for my dad to bless the food so we could dig in.

My mom's hand locked with mine, and naturally, I reached for Morgan's beside me. As our fingers connected I felt like all eyes were on me, so I closed mine to avoid their looks. "Dear Heavenly Father, on this day of Thanksgiving we want to thank you for your provision, for the hands that prepared this meal, for our children making it home safely, and for our friends." I peeled one eye open to look at my dad as he continued, "May we all feel the love that surrounds us as we enjoy this meal today. In Jesus's name we pray. Amen."

I uttered Amen, and when it was time to release Morgan's hand I slowly let it go. Looking to her, I mouthed, "Everything okay?" And she nodded gently. "Good."

The conversation was going well with my sister describing her latest travels. Although, I could only half listen because I was working myself into a food coma. With casual looks toward Morgan, I couldn't have been happier than in that moment. Good food, a beautiful woman beside me, and my family around me.

As my dad's prayer suggested, I was feeling the love that surrounded me.

"It's just that you can't find a church home on the road like that, can you?" I looked between my mama and my sister as my sister slightly rolled her eyes.

My eyebrows peaked because I just knew the conversation was about to get interesting, but I hoped it wouldn't become completely unhinged as Morgan sat astonished.

"Mama," Natalie sounded exhausted already, "I told you most of the time I find someplace to worship." Then she mumbled, "Just might not be every Sunday." She pointed her eyes toward me and said, "And what about Cody?" She nudged her chin my way. "You haven't asked him about his church attendance yet."

I felt Morgan's leg brush up against mine as she adjusted in her seat. When I looked down at her plate, I saw her hand circling the fork around it, but she wasn't indulging how I expected.

"You're right, Nat." My mama turned from my sister to me. "Did you find a church home yet?"

I shook my head. "Not yet, but I will. I've been trying out a few." I explained to Morgan, "My mama is a deaconess. She and my dad have been members of the same church for as long as I can remember."

My dad chimed in, "Over thirty years now."

"You know, it's not that hard." Then my mama's eyes were on Morgan, and I leaned forward to break her stare to protect Morgan from whatever my mama was about to ask next. "Morgan, I'm sure you have a church home, right?"

Morgan cleared her throat, and I watched her as she considered a response. "No, actually, I don't."

"People fall away from God's grace all the time. They get wrapped up in their lives. With work." My mama's gaze was traveling around the table until her eyes landed on Morgan's. "Or they get lost in a relationship and forget the one relationship that matters most."

Morgan's fork dropped to the table, and she quickly uttered, "Sorry about that." Her gaze turning toward me before she quickly looked away and found a spot on the beige wall to stare at.

"It's critical that we all maintain a good relationship with God. Fellowship with each other and keep the people we love uplifted."

Then as if she hadn't just scolded each of us, she asked, "Anyone ready for pie?"

I stood from the table, grabbing my plate as I did. "Do you want to keep that?" I asked Morgan, but she shook her head. "I'll help you Mama," I said, walking toward the kitchen with our plates. Waiting for my mama to join me, I paced the length of the counter. "What was that?" I whispered when she entered the kitchen.

"That?" she said nonchalantly. "What was wrong with what I said?"

"She's a guest, Mama," I reminded her. "The last thing we should be trying to do is make her feel uncomfortable."

She retorted, "Uncomfortable?" Then she shook her head. "Even if she is just a friend, I'd like to think you'd like the people around you to be covered by God's grace." Her arms crossed over her chest. "I want you and Nat to be, and anyone associated with you." She tilted her head to the side as I paused in front of her. "What's wrong with that?"

I sighed. "Nothing, I guess. But…" I couldn't find the words to tell her to be easy with Morgan. To explain her fragile state without giving up too much information that wasn't mine to provide. "Just can we chill a bit, Sister Felix?"

With her hand in the air, she promised, "Alright, son. I'll *chill*. Help me plate this pie."

Morgan didn't say much more that night despite everyone trying to keep the conversation light. Finally, I asked, "Are you ready?" And for the first time that night she looked excited as she nodded her head. "Okay, c'mon." I announced to my family, "I'm going to get Morgan home. I'll be back this weekend and go to church with you, Mama." She looked very pleased by the offer, and I made sure to pull Natalie in on it too. "Nat, you'll stick around for church, right?"

She shot daggers my way before replying, "Sure, I'll be here." Her look went to Morgan as if she was going to suggest something, but I gave her a tight-lipped stare that dared her not to even try.

Morgan was quiet in the car, and I could understand because the amount of food I ate had drained my energy. I was ready to get home and crash, but when I looked at Morgan with her fidgeting hand, I realized that may not have been her situation. "Did you have a good time tonight?"

After a long delay, she said, "I am trying to determine how to best say what I need to say." My hands tensed around the wheel, because as much as I wanted her to tell me something sweet, and kind, her tone indicated it wouldn't be.

"Whatever it is, just say it how you feel."

"Okay," she said as her mouth closed. "I would have never expected that you would share something I told you in confidence with your family."

I scoured the night, quickly trying to recall what might

have been said. Then I remembered she was in the kitchen with Natalie and my mama, alone, for a while. "Was it something they said to you in the kitchen?" She shook her head. "Then when?"

She cleared her throat. "At the table, about church. And a relationship with God being more important than one with someone else."

"Morgan, I didn't talk to my family about your ex at all. Not about your spirituality, nothing," I clarified. "At most, I gave them a rundown of how we knew each other, freshman year in college, then reacquainting a couple of months ago." I declared, "That's it."

She groaned, "Are you sure? You didn't tell her anything? She just came up with that on her own?"

I was more concerned about my mama asking us about our non-existent church membership than the spiel she gave afterward. "I'm positive." We were both silent until I pulled in front of her townhouse. Looking up at the stairs, I considered where I stood with Morgan. I was at the bottom step, at most, and making it to the top felt like a feat only Rocky could accomplish.

The sniffle I heard beside me broke my stare away from the stairs. "Morgan," I said, finding her hand in the dark and holding on to it with everything I had. "Tell me what's going on."

"Each day when I think I'm further from the hurt, the pain, I am reminded just how much I was drug through the mud. How much I came out of this and I'm still trying to remove the stains of my descent into the pit."

I rubbed a thumb against her wrist and although I wanted to offer her comforting words, I was at a loss. I had never experienced anyone who was recovering from a tumultuous relationship. Although the words my mom spoke to us were how we got to that moment with her in tears in the passenger seat of my car, those were the words I referenced. "My mama may have been right about one thing. We need to uplift those around us. And although this process to get beyond the pit may feel exhausting, and you may want to throw in the towel, I'm going to pray that your strength is renewed. That you'll soon have peace and understanding."

Once her sniffles subsided, I stepped out of the car and walked her to the front door. She was standing in the doorway wiping her face. "Thank you for the invite." Then she started, "I'm sorry—"

"No need to apologize, honestly." I smiled. "Thanks for joining me." I opened my arms wide, and she walked into them easily. The hug was briefer than I'd want it to be, but I knew she had a long way to go before she could offer anything more.

Chapter Fifteen

MORGAN

I couldn't imagine Elijah spending his time thinking of me. Not like I had thought of him. It wasn't like my hand was hovering over his name in my phone to text him and ask how he was doing. Or that I wanted to call from a blocked number just to hear his voice.

No, my thoughts didn't linger there. I didn't miss him. Or even the idea of him. But it didn't matter because he was plaguing my thoughts. He was constantly on my mind. Although none of the thoughts were kind, his presence in my memories was still unwelcome.

In some ways, I wanted to know his Thanksgiving was ruined by a memory of us. Or that his parents asked about me, and where I was, and he had to awkwardly describe our breakup. That he had to admit that he was trash.

In reality though, I doubted any of that happened. Knowing him, he went to Thanksgiving with a clear conscience, ate the food, and left just as happy as he was when he arrived.

I hated that I spent not only Thanksgiving spiraling into deep thoughts of him, but that entire weekend. By Monday morning, I was exhausted. Overwhelmed and thinking of all the ways I could finally rid myself of him. Of every single thought of him, of the good and the bad, the terrible and appalling.

I didn't want his name to be whispered in my thoughts when I thought of all the good things I could be experiencing. If I could only trust again.

Then Cody's prayer, his sweet, adorable words whispered to God's ears. That peace that he requested on my behalf—more than I wanted anything else in the world—I wanted that.

Each time a thought of Elijah or the pain he caused snuck into my mind, I whispered the same prayer, "God, give me peace and understanding."

I was in the middle of reciting it again after looking at my hectic schedule for the day. Because our office was closed for Thanksgiving and the day after, Monday came with more force than a typical Monday.

If I could have snuck away to the coffee shop, taking the long route as I walked there, I would have hopped from my seat and skipped out the front door anticipating I'd bump into Cody. The fact that he was starting to become the person I imagined when everything was falling apart spoke volumes. I didn't want to ignore it. I didn't want to discount it because I had an issue with… I cleared my head again. "Peace and understanding, God."

"Morgan." I heard a light tap on the wall of my cubicle.

"Ms. Moore," followed by another knock that made me stop my fingers from tapping away mid-sentence.

"Yes?" I said as I turned to look at the blue-eyed, blond-haired company favorite, *James*. I didn't even notice the vase in his hands until he stretched it toward me with a blank stare.

"Flower delivery for you." Then he looked down at the vase with a smirk on his face. "Not sure if we missed the first delivery, but it looks…" his head wagged side to side before he told me, "It looks wilted." I grabbed the vase from his hands and had a similar reaction as his. Trying to determine what it was, and why someone would have delivered a flower that had already died. Seemed like a cruel joke. Momentarily, I imagined Elijah doing something cruel like that to get under my skin. That was quickly dismissed because even if he wanted to, he probably didn't know how to order flowers. At least that's how it seemed all the years we spent together.

'Thanks," I finally said to James's retreating back.

I plucked the card from the vase and opened it quickly so that I could return to the brief I was typing.

A lotus flower cannot receive moisture after it's been cut from the plant. The wilting flower may not hold beauty when it's disconnected, but the strength it shows to grow through the mud is much more powerful anyway.

The words danced in my head as I read them over and over again. Then his name transcribed at the end brought a huge grin to my face.

Cody Felix

"Wow," I mouthed. The wilting flower empowered me in a way that I felt unstoppable. Like I could make it through the day of briefs, meetings, and long hours just because of the words scribbled on a card, the leaves of a flower that looked to be weeping. I scooted the vase to the corner of my desk, and every so often, I'd look over to the vase and pause as the space in my chest swelled.

The mid-day meeting that extended well past the one-hour block on my calendar didn't bother me. Not when I was excited about making it back to my desk to look at the *wilted* flower. As Christina walked beside me, my legs hurrying to carry me to my cubicle, she noted, "You seem to be in a really good mood today." She asked, "Must have been an amazing Thanksgiving. You spent it with…" she tapped her chin, "his family, right?" She smiled but her head was tilted to the side like she suspected something more.

"Cody. Right. It wasn't bad." I frowned. "Not entirely."

Through a laugh, she said, "I mean, meeting people's family can always be strange. A little awkward too." She fanned her hand in the air. "Not like I'd know from personal experience, as it never gets that far. But I could imagine."

I laughed along with her and when I was in front of my desk, I gazed at the corner of my cubicle. "Oh, what's that?" She leaned forward at the sight of the vase, and as she peered in she said, "Looks like it's at the end of its, time whatever it is," a look of disgust on her face as she looked from the vase to me. "But you look happy." She tilted her head sideways, her eyes dancing around the office space. "It's been a minute since I've seen you this happy."

My shoulders went up to my neck as she leaned into me and wrapped her arms around my shoulders. Then she outstretched them and examined my face a little harder. "If

Love is Patient

wilted flowers are making you this happy, who am I to judge?"

I laughed as she walked back to her office.

I considered leaving the vase in the office, but like a new pet, I always wanted it around me. At the end of the day, I slung my computer bag over one shoulder, my purse over the other, and carried the vase in my hands as I exited to my car.

I placed it carefully in the passenger seat and hoped it wouldn't fall over as I drove across town to my house. Had I not been watching it carefully as I navigated into my parking spot, I would have seen him sitting at the top of my steps. I probably would have even backed out quickly and found someplace, anyplace else to go. There was no need for Elijah to be in front of my house at the end of my day.

But it was too late, I was climbing out of the car by the time I noticed him. I balanced the vase in one hand and shuffled through my purse looking for my keys with the other. "What are you smiling about?" was the first thing out of his mouth, as if he still possessed the right to even ask me anything.

I didn't dignify his question with a response; instead, I just asked, "What are you doing here?" as I eased past him and stood in front of the door. I kept my distance but stood firm, waiting for him to speak before I opened it.

"Are those flowers?" he asked another question that went unanswered as he looked at the vase in my hand. With a low growl, he said, "Already got somebody buying you flowers." He scoffed, and that's when I smelled the liquor on his breath and knew whatever landed him on my front steps wouldn't let him leave easily.

"You need to leave," I told him with a forceful tone anyway.

His face turned further into a scowl, and I noticed how red his eyes were. Usually when he drank his eyes didn't turn red. *Was he crying?* I closed my eyes quickly before opening them, ready to tell him to leave again, because I couldn't let myself get sucked into caring for him. But my phone was ringing in my purse, and for some reason I decided to answer it.

One look at the name on the screen, and the anger that had started to build up with Elijah being on my steps was easing away. I even managed to smile as I answered.

"Morgan." His voice was calming and had a way of easing my mind. Erasing any doubt about everything else going on. "Did you get a delivery today?"

I looked down at my hand and smiled. "I did," I told him.

The phone tumbled from my grip, and the vase went crashing into the ground. Glass shattered all over the steps, and I felt a throbbing in my back as Elijah stood in front of me with his hand against my chest. "You think you are just about to disrespect me like that?" He yelled, "You think I care about those little flowers, and whoever it is that gave them to you?"

Each of his words was punctuated with a flicker of saliva as he growled into my ear. Our bodies dangerously close, I held my breath and just prayed silently, "God, just make him leave. Please." My eyes were closed as I waited for whatever it was he needed to say to me to be tossed from his lips.

"Ten years. And you stopped answering my calls. Haven't checked on me." He stared into my eyes. "My mama asking what I did to break us up. Like it was my fault."

"Elijah? What?" I said, opening my eyes and straining to focus on anything besides the red of his eyes, the stench of his breath, and the warmth of his body.

To think there was once a time when I craved the warmth he gave me. A time when I would have loved to be just that close to him, looking at him adoringly as he whispered sweetly into my ears. *When did we go from that to this?*

"It doesn't even matter because apparently, you've replaced me." He laughed and I felt his hand sliding from my chest to my neck, and my breathing halted in my throat. "Just know he'll never be able to treat you like me."

I wanted to say, *"Because he'd treat me better,"* but the words wouldn't form as the breath was leaving my body. I was gasping for air as I watched him, pleading that he'd just let go. That he'd leave me alone.

God please, I thought as tears stung my eyes.

Chapter Sixteen

CODY

Spending Sunday morning at church with my family only made me miss Morgan more. The couple of days since seeing her felt like an eternity, especially since all I wanted to do was wrap my arms around her. To let her know there wasn't anything I wouldn't do to ensure she was okay.

During the sermon though, when the preacher said, "God is the source of our comfort, so that we can be of comfort to others," I couldn't hear the rest of his message.

When my mama asked, "Now aren't you glad you joined us today?" I nodded because I was glad I joined them. I needed to feel God's comfort—because Morgan needed it. "Me too, son," she said as she wrapped her arms around me. Standing in my mama's embrace, I even considered that Morgan couldn't run home when she was hurting. That home was the last place she wanted to be. I couldn't imagine not being able to turn to my mama, or my dad, my sister even.

It wasn't until after Sunday dinner and the drive back to Greensboro that I decided I wanted to send Morgan a gift, something to let her know I admired her for what she was powering through. Despite her circumstances, she was still standing.

The lotus flower was the first thing I thought of, and as I called the local florist she explained why they didn't have any for delivery, "You do know that it wilts almost immediately, right?"

"Yes," I told her as she continued. "But is there anywhere I can find it locally?" As she gave me a name, I scribbled it on a piece of paper and called them immediately. Although it was an odd request for the botanical garden, they agreed to let me buy a single bloom.

After managing the rest, I was able to hire a delivery person to take it to her job. Through all my classes, I hoped that she'd gotten the vase, and the card was still attached. Hiring a delivery guy off the internet was also new to me. But if she was able to smile, the effort was worth it.

By the end of the day though, when I hadn't heard from her despite the delivery guy telling me the task was complete, I grew skeptical.

I could hear the smile when she answered my call, and all was well in the world. Until it wasn't. I heard the phone as it tumbled, and the sound of glass shattering, then I thought I was going to levitate out of my body as I heard a man's voice come over the phone.

Thankfully, I was already in my car, headed home, and only minutes from Morgan's house. It was the time she should have been at home, and I didn't know what I'd be rolling up on, but I had to get to her. I turned my car around at the light and headed in her direction.

I sped through her neighborhood, navigating parked cars and pedestrians as I tried to race to her. I threw the car in park, swung my door open, and climbed the stairs by two until I was beside her, and Elijah. *Elijah.*

"I don't think you want to do that." I stepped to him and waited until his arm released her neck before I spoke again. First, checking on Morgan, "You okay?" I looked at the glass, shattered beside her, the phone a few steps down, and the look of shock on her face.

"Hold up," I heard him say from behind me. The platform of her steps growing increasingly smaller as the three of us tried to fight for space. "This ain't even about you, bruh."

Elijah looked like he'd seen the bottom of a bottle—with red eyes, wrinkled clothes, and a stench I couldn't even stomach. "It's not, but whatever you have going on, doesn't concern *her* either." I stood with a wide stance, challenging him to make a move.

His eyes widened before his head fell back. "This dude?" His finger went into my chest. "You?" Then his eyes shot a glance at Morgan. "All this time you tried to make me think I was a fool back then when I said he was trying to smash." He snickered, "I'm supposed to believe he just showed up after all these years?"

I didn't care how he pulled the story together, or what he thought of me, but the sound of Morgan sniffling behind me rattled my core. "Pretty sure she asked you to leave," I said firmly.

"Oh, don't worry about me." He cleared his throat and spit on the ground between us before he backed away. He said, "You can have her," like she was his to give away.

I watched him wobble down the stairs and walk to a car nearby. I didn't move until his license plate was far down the road, far enough that I couldn't read it anymore. Then I turned to Morgan and asked, "Where are your keys?"

Her shoulders were slumped as she looked down at the vase, the wilted flower sitting near her foot. "I'll clean that up. Let me get your keys so you can get inside." When she didn't move, I looked at her purse. "Mind if I get them out for you?" She shook her head, and I dug through her purse until I felt the coldness from the metal of a keychain.

I opened the door and stepped aside so she could walk in. "I'll grab a trash bag and a broom to clean up the mess." I walked beyond her to the kitchen and grabbed what I needed to start cleaning. I grabbed the phone and placed it in her hands then got to work.

Each piece of shattered glass enraged me more. The flower that should have represented Morgan's strength was lying withered on the step and felt like a mockery of my sentiment. My fists clenched and opened a few times before I walked through her door again. Disposing of the mess, I found her in the kitchen leaning against the counter. Her shoulders were shaking, and tears were streaming down her face.

I was careful not to touch her, standing a few feet away as I asked, "Morgan, are you okay?"

The dark makeup from her eyes dripped down her cheek, the red lipstick smeared across her mouth, and her eyes were bloodshot. *She wasn't okay.* And I didn't need to hear her whisper "No" to confirm it.

"Can I hold you?" She nodded and slowly walked into my arms. I felt her chest heaving, her sniffles as she sobbed, and after minutes of that I walked us to her couch. Sat her down softly, stooped down, and removed the shoes from her feet. Then I sat down and let her rest her head on my shoulder.

Silence felt like the most appropriate response to what happened to her that evening. I started processing what I witnessed, and felt the weight of the *what-ifs* falling on my shoulders. What if I didn't call her? What if I didn't get there to convince him to release his hold around her neck? What if he turned on me?

I closed my eyes and thought *Thank God*, that none of that happened.

"Cody?" I heard her say with a raspy voice, "How'd you know to come?"

I explained, "The phone never hung up. I could hear him talking to you, the glass as it shattered." I cringed as the sound replayed. "I was on my way home and got here as fast as I could."

She sat up, looked into my eyes, and placed a hand to my cheek. The coolness from her palm relieving the heat that had started to settle in my bones from the anger. "Thank you."

I placed my hand over hers and said, "I can stay as long as you need to make sure you are comfortable." Then I considered maybe she wanted to be alone. "Or I can leave if you need some time to yourself." I didn't think Elijah was bold enough to return, but in his state, anything was possible.

"Stay," she whispered as she leaned forward, "Please stay." Her lips connected with mine as she crawled into my lap. My hands wrapped around her waist as her tongue slid into my mouth. The moisture on her face as it brushed against mine reminded me that we couldn't go there. Not then. I pulled apart slowly and rested my head on hers. With my eyes closed, I whispered, "I didn't rush over here to help you with hopes you'd fall for me. I came to make sure whoever the man was I heard on the phone would not hurt you. Knowing it's Elijah, I want to make sure *he* never hurts you again." I sighed. "But we can't do this right now."

I opened my eyes as she crawled from my lap. Her lip tucked between her teeth she nodded. "You're right," she looked away and said, "I shouldn't be trying to make love to you when I'm still reeling from everything that happened today, and the past few months." Admittedly, my mind stuck on the words *make love to you*. I didn't realize she was on her feet, pacing in front of me, until I heard, "I think I'll be fine. I need to process what happened. Maybe you should leave."

I stood in front of her path until she stopped. "No matter the time, if you need anything, call me, okay?" I reached for her hand and pulled it to my mouth as it rested softly in my palm. After a kiss to her wrist, I led us to the front door where I sternly said, "Lock up."

She mouthed, "Thank you," before I walked down the steps.

Chapter Seventeen

MORGAN

There was once a time when I was a regular churchgoer. So regularly that I didn't need to stand in my closet staring at clothes in hopes of finding a church-appropriate outfit. I always had something ready to go.

When I woke up that morning I decided it was time for me to get back into church, to feel close to God, and covered by His grace. I remember how I felt going to church when I first started in college. It was the people—kind and welcoming—that I enjoyed the most. I couldn't compare it to much because we didn't go to church often when I was a kid.

We were what my grandmother called CME People—attending church only on Christmas, Mother's Day, and Easter. Despite her warning that we needed to be in church more often, Mama refused. She told us if we prayed we'd be alright.

Clearly, that wasn't the case for her. At least not from my

Love is Patient

perspective. Maybe she could have used church a few times a month, and not quarterly.

In college I didn't plan to increase my attendance, but there was a church member on campus inviting students to service and I decided, "why not?"

That was the church I found myself in that morning. Inside, the pews were packed and many of the people looked like me when I was in college. I found a seat in the middle of the church next to a nice older woman. One of the seasoned saints with a big hat covering her face. I sat down and whispered, "Good morning," as I adjusted in the seat, and her hand went to my knee as she returned the greeting. Already I felt lighter than when I walked in.

There were church announcements, which I listened to intently trying to stay focused. Then the choir stood and started to sing, "Speak to my heart, Lord," and my eyes closed tight as the words poured over me. I could hear the claps from those around me, the beat of the drum, the piano keys with each note, and even a tambourine off to my side. Eventually my mouth began to sing along, reciting the words along with the choir. My hands rubbed up and down my arms, and I swayed back and forth as a chill overtook my body.

As the instruments faded and the voices stopped, I opened my eyes and saw the pastor standing behind his podium. A concerned look on his face as he scanned the audience. "Let's pray." I bowed my head and listened. "Heavenly Father, we are gathered in your place this morning. To hear a word from you. Speak to our hearts, oh Lord, allow us to remember that you are near." I heard him sigh before he continued, "God, someone here today is hurting. In pain, and heartbroken. I know that you can and you will mend their broken pieces." My head tilted up, and my eyes landed on the pastor as he continued, "Allow them to know that if they can't trust anyone else, Lord, they can trust you." As he and the church repeated, "Amen," I sat speechless. *God's handiwork* was all I could think as the sermon began.

"Today, I planned to preach a different sermon, but I'm being led to the book of Corinthians. Turn your Bibles with me to First Corinthians Chapter 13." He began to read the scriptures, and the words were as sweet as the melody the choir had just sung. "Love is patient, love is kind." I watched as his eyes went from the Bible to those of us in the pews. "The greatest gift God gives to us is love. As He loves us, we should remember to love others." He held up a finger. "And know that others should love us the same."

Without notice, I felt a tear trickle down my cheek. One after the other, the tears were flowing as I listened to the pastor. I felt a hand outstretched beside me, and when I turned there was a tissue waiting for me. "Thank you," I said with a gentle smile as I dabbed at my face.

"You are God's creation. You were masterfully crafted by the Father, and there should not be a single person on this earth who can tell you that you are anything less than amazing. God made no mistake when He made you." More tears fell. By the time he said, "The doors of the church are open, if you want to be in a place where we exercise God's love, join us," I was a sobbing mess. His arms were outstretched, and the call felt significant, relevant, like I wanted my feet to move, but I stayed rooted in my seat.

Until the seasoned saint leaned over, her hat shielding us from the stares of anyone else as she said, "Baby, if you want to go, you don't have to walk alone." Her hand slid into mine and I looked at our fingers interlaced as the people started clapping for those who were already standing at the altar.

I looked at the woman and nodded. Standing from my seat, I thought my legs would feel powerless, shaky, as I took those steps. They were everything but. My back was straight as I stood in front of the altar, the woman's hand gently on my back for support, but I was standing.

The pastor began to speak but was overpowered by the woman's voice in my ear that said, "If there is anything you want to lay at the altar, go ahead, baby."

I didn't know exactly what it was she was referring to, but I closed my eyes and said quietly, "God, here I stand. I'm releasing this pain, the hurt, the anger, the resentment. I'm allowing your love to embody me completely." As I whispered, "Amen," I felt the woman's hand rubbing my back and when I turned, it was time for us to return to our seats. Before we both sat, I turned and wrapped my arms around her, and she embraced me.

In my ear, she whispered, "Baby, you might not feel like you are winning this battle, but God never loses." Then we both sat as the choir sang one more song.

By the time we were dismissed, I was ready to beeline to my car. My face was probably a hot mess, makeup smeared all over, tear stains, and red eyes. I didn't want to hang around for the meet and greet, so I made my way out the door, but knew as soon as I was outside I'd be back.

The seasoned saint was right. There was a battle I felt like I was losing, and as I navigated my neighborhood I was reminded of it. My hands tensed around the wheel as the memory of finding Elijah on my doorstep replayed. As it had been all week. My feet slowly pressed the brake, and I slowly drove to my parking spot. Each time I returned home it'd take me pausing in the car, examining my surroundings before I had the nerve to climb out. To walk up the steps, to get inside my house, lock the doors, and not leave until the next day.

The memory had paralyzed me. Made me fearful of my *own* house. As I sat in the car, ready to put myself through the mental anguish, I prayed, "God, I need you to fight this battle for me." As I looked at the steps I said, "Protect me from Elijah, his words, his hands, his ways."

I opened the car door, and the walk to my steps didn't feel like I was walking through wet cement. My shoulders weren't sagging, and my heart wasn't racing. I made it to my front door without constantly checking over my shoulder, and by the time I was in my house I was able to sigh a breath of relief.

The anxiety was gone.

Parts of the sermon stuck out to me as I climbed out of my clothes. "Love is kind." And I remembered Cody and how he swooped in to help. How since we saw each other in the coffee shop he had shown nothing but kindness toward me.

I laughed as I considered the timing. Then I remembered something I heard from the pastor, years earlier, "God's timing is perfect."

I believed it was, that God would send me a man who would be perfect for me, when the time was right. I just couldn't help but think about my mama, and all the men she had in her life. She went from abusive guy to abusive guy without even taking a breath in between.

In the middle of my closet, half-dressed, I took a vow to myself. Before I moved on to another guy, I'd fall back in love with God, then myself. I looked up to the ceiling and said, "I know you never lose God, and I can't wait to see you win."

Chapter Eighteen

CODY

Waking up Christmas morning at my parents' house was nothing like it was when we were kids. Although I could smell the aroma of bacon wafting into my room from the kitchen, Natalie wasn't rushing in telling me we had to get out to the tree.

As my mama warned, "Until I get some grandbabies there won't be many gifts under that tree." I took her threat to heart and hoped that one day I could deliver on her request. The one woman I even slightly considered a possibility wasn't talking to me. Not that I expected her to because when I left her house that night, I was committed to giving her space. To let her work through all the chaos Elijah was subjecting her to. I wanted her to be free of him and thoughts of him without me crowding her space.

I couldn't lie though, not talking to her, hearing her voice, and especially not seeing her made each day that passed harder.

For Christmas, I would have loved to wake up to her, exchange gifts, and indulge in all types of food. Since that wasn't the case, I was left wondering how she was spending Christmas and prayed it was full of joy, and no pain.

A loud knock at my door, and a loud-mouthed Natalie, interrupted my thoughts of Morgan. "Hey, let's go help Mama finish up this breakfast so we can eat," she said, rubbing her belly.

"Alright, give me a second," I told her as I untangled myself from the comforter and walked to the bathroom.

After my morning routine, I walked past the large Christmas tree and into the kitchen. The laughter that rang out as my dad twirled my mama around brought a smile to my face, and my thoughts back to Morgan. One day, I'd love to have what my parents had.

"Mama, while you dance, how about me and Nat wrap up breakfast?" Natalie was already standing over the stove with the eggs. "What's left?"

"Check the biscuits." She pointed toward the stove as my dad spun her around again.

The biscuits were finished and as I pulled them from the oven, I asked my sister, "Done with those eggs?" My stomach grumbled as the smells started to overwhelm the kitchen. "I can't wait to eat."

I pulled orange juice from the fridge and told my parents, "Go ahead and sit down so we can eat."

Before they did, I watched my dad kiss my mom like his kids weren't in the room. Natalie cleared her throat as I looked away. "What?" he asked with a grin, "How do you think the two of you got here?" My mama was the only one chuckling at his little joke.

Finally, we were all seated around the table as my dad recited grace. I looked at the seat beside me, the one where Morgan sat for Thanksgiving, and felt a tug in my chest. "How is she?" I looked up at my mama with a wrinkled brow. "Morgan."

I hesitated with how much I wanted to reveal about Morgan. She was very clear that what she shared with me was not to be discussed with anyone else, and I respected that. But it was a critical piece to them understanding her. "I hope she's well." I continued eating with my eyes set on my plate.

"You hope?" my dad responded. I looked up to him and nodded my head. "Still exercising that patience?"

I sighed, "Yeah."

"What's that, Carter?" my mama asked, looking my dad's way.

Instead of letting him tell his rendition, I said, "Morgan isn't ready to receive love yet." I carefully selected the next words, "I'm doing my best to give her space right now."

She looked from my dad to me before saying, "Does your definition of space mean you aren't checking on her?" I wagged my head and she scoffed. "Please don't tell me that's the advice your daddy gave you." She shot a side-eye toward him as I shook my head.

"Oh no, babe, I told him to be patient. That eventually everything will fall into place when it is supposed to. I didn't tell the man to stop talking to her." He frowned.

"Good." My mama nodded. "That wouldn't be wise advice. No matter what she's going through, she should be reminded that you care. You need to check in on her and prove that although she's not ready, you haven't moved on." I rested the fork on my plate as I listened. "Pour into her. One day the holes in her heart will be sealed and what you have been pouring in won't seep out." I was listening to her words as I would the gospel. "Eventually she'll be able to consume love again, and out of the abundance that you've given her it will flow out to those around her." She smirked. "And hopefully that'll include you." She looked to Natalie and my dad then back to me and said, "But we love without expectations of it being returned." Her eyes were soft when she asked, "Do you understand?"

"Yes," I told her, "I do."

For the first time in a couple of weeks, I sat down with my phone in my hand and decided I needed to take my mom's advice. I tapped on Morgan's name and started a text message.

Cody: Merry Christmas, I hope that you are doing well.

I didn't expect a message back, although I was watching my screen for the sign that she was replying. The vibration in my hand startled me, especially when I saw it was a phone call from Morgan. "Hello?" I quickly said with a smile on my face.

"Merry Christmas, Cody." I could hear her smiling, and if that was the only gift I received on Christmas it would have been an amazing day.

"How are you?" I asked, hoping her response didn't remind her of any negative memories.

She paused, then thoughtfully she said, "You know, I think there are a few ways I would have preferred to spend Christmas, but I'm good."

I laughed, "Oh yeah. How's that?"

"Honestly?" I uttered a quiet response. "I would have loved to see you." Christmas at my parents' house was wrapping up, and I was about to stand up, wish them well, and go wherever she was just to give Morgan what she wanted, but she said, "Christmas with the bestie and her family isn't too bad though."

"Ava?" I asked.

"Yes, Ava." Then she joked, "Didn't know if you'd remember her."

Although my interaction with her at homecoming was brief, Morgan spoke about her often. "Ava should be happy to know that you mention her name casually at least a couple of times a day." I laughed. "Where are you?" Morgan didn't share where Ava was from, or where she lived even. I just knew she wasn't in Greensboro, even though Morgan would have loved for her to be there.

"We are in Atlanta with her family." The thought that she still didn't go home to spend the holidays with her own family pained me.

I could hear people in the background, lots of laughter, and I was glad she at least wasn't alone. "I won't keep you…" I started, although I didn't want the call to end.

"Yeah, I should get back to the festivities. Her mama is pulling out more dessert. Although I'm stuffed, I guess I'll make room for a little something."

"Enjoy that." Before I hung up I said, "Hey, Morgan."

"Yes, Cody."

"I'm glad you're doing well."

"Me too." She repeated, "Me too."

Chapter Nineteen

MORGAN

I made it through the holidays without any major breakdowns. For me, that was a win. I wasn't on a new year, new me kick. Not exactly. But I did promise to get back to what I loved. Before Elijah derailed all my plans.

It had been years since the last time I rocked a leotard and the soft leather shoes that I once thought I'd never take off. It was past time for me to get back to a studio. I scrolled through options online and was considering what a commitment to a class would look like. What time I'd have to dedicate to lessons, especially with a hectic schedule. Then as I looked at the times, I decided no matter how and when it happened, I'd make it work. I had to.

I opened a notebook and scribbled a few options, some studios that opened since the last time I danced, and others that had been open for years. Then the last I wrote on the notepad was one I frequented often, a class on campus. Just a different teacher. I put a small star next to that one and smiled.

"Morgan," I heard the sing-song voice of Christina behind me, "Busy?" I looked from my screen to her and shook my head. "Ballet?" She leaned against my desk and crossed her arms. "Are you trying to go to another performance?"

I cringed and told her, "No," with a wag of my head I said, "I'm trying to perform."

As if I said there was a tiger behind her, she gasped, "What?"

"You know I used to dance, right?" I couldn't believe that it wasn't common knowledge. When I was dancing, it was something I talked about often to any and everyone who would listen. There weren't many people who hadn't heard of my dream to move to New York and perform on stage with a famous dance company.

With a look over my shoulder, she said, "So you are going to start again?" She didn't sound as enthused as I felt. I was overjoyed at the thought of dancing again. "When will you have time?"

"I'll have to find time."

She shrugged her shoulder. "I can't knock that. Never too late to live your dreams." I hung onto those words, and when she asked, "But why'd you stop dancing in the first place?" I cringed. "Sorry, is it personal?"

I shook my head, because although I was proud of the days that go by without a single thought of Elijah, I knew it wasn't realistic to not think of him ever. "Well," I started, and looked behind her to the lawyers that were walking our way, "Sadly, I let my ex convince me I wasn't good enough."

She pulled back like my words were fire and she didn't

want to be burned. I could relate. Thinking of how he tortured me about not spending time with him, being too busy for practice, rehearsals, eventually, I gave in. I should have fought for my dreams though. Or as Ava kindly told me, I should have dropped Elijah instead.

"And what about the new guy? I assume he's much more supportive."

I scrunched my nose and looked down at my notebook to the studio marked with a star. "I'm not exactly dating him right now."

I knew Christina had work to do, her calendar was busier than mine, but still she stood right in my cubicle to hear the story about me and Cody. "I've gone back to church, and right now I'm not trying to focus on any other relationships other than the one with God and myself."

She pursed her lips and nodded her head. "I love that for you. And if you are determined to dance, I could be looking at the next Misty Copeland."

The thought alone eased my worry about joining a class. About being an out of practice, much older woman trying to chase her dreams. Ones that an expiration date associated with my physical ability. If I couldn't bend and fold, twist and turn like I used to, my dream may end up a fond memory of what once was before it slowly chipped away.

"There's only one way to find out if that's even possible," I told her as I clicked back into the studio I once frequented.

"That's what I'm talking about," she scoffed. "Get your butt back in there." She winked before walking away.

After registering, I thought about everything I needed to purchase and got right on that, ordering everything I needed online.

I'd been on campus for homecoming and other events

over the years, but walking on campus in my ballet gear made me feel like I was still in college. Still excited about the prospect to dance professionally. Madly in love with the art, and the man I thought would have been supportive of me. I was headed toward the recreation center, where some of the students hosted an after-hours class.

Walking through the front door, I looked around at the women against the bar stretching and became a ball of emotions—excited about dancing again, but nervous to be amongst the younger women who likely didn't have a ten-year hiatus from dancing.

"Come on in," I heard someone say from the front of the room. "We'll be starting shortly."

I dropped my bag and peeled out of the layers of clothes I was wearing until I had only my tank top and leggings on. I sat against the mirrors and pulled on my shoes. I scanned the line of women before finding an empty spot near the bar where I began stretching.

The way my body flexed and responded like it was back in familiar territory was welcoming. I wish I could have said the same about the class. I was obviously out of practice, and it showed. It didn't matter though because I continued, and when it was over the instructor stood beside me and asked, "Has it been a while?" I nodded. "Don't worry, it'll come back to you." She winked and I hoped she was right.

Walking across campus again, I thought about the only person I still knew on campus and wondered if he was somewhere tucked inside his office. Or if I'd be lucky enough to bump into him.

I wasn't.

I made it to my car without an encounter with Cody, but I didn't let that discourage me because I was sure I'd hear from him. He sent at least two texts a day—one to tell me good morning and another to tell me goodnight.

I appreciated both, mainly the fact that he was checking in with me often. That regardless of what I was ready for I knew he was there, and that gave me comfort.

Chapter Twenty

CODY

Sometimes students needed help. Typically, I didn't mind staying late after class to help them. But with an evening class, staying late meant I was rolling into darkness before I could get home. Still, when Trevor, the kid who reminded me of myself, asked, "Could you just help me understand…" I held the sigh I wanted to release.

"Of course," I said, looking at the paper he outstretched. "In this scenario…" I stared as his eyes focused on the paper. "You know what, let me draw it on the board." I took out an Expo marker and started describing the factors related to social isolation created by *social media*. "It can be hard to identify," I explained as I put the cap back on, "but with thoughtful design, you can create solutions that still solve the problem and don't become the problem."

As soon as I saw his smile and head nod, I was ready to leave. Then he said, "But how do we even measure the impact, or negative impacts?" My shoulders slumped and I wanted to tell him I had a game to get home to watch. But solving the social dilemma was why I was teaching the course. Students like Trevor were the reason I was at A&T.

I eased the cap back off the marker and began to explain, talking quicker than I would have during a normal class. "How about that?" I asked as he stood looking more bewildered than when he asked the first question. I laughed. "Listen, this isn't something you'll get overnight. It'll take time, practice, digging deep into the resource material." I reminded him, "Starting with that may be helpful actually."

"Right." He held out his hand and I shook it. "Thanks for taking a little time with me. I appreciate it."

"Of course." I smiled and waited for him to leave the classroom before I followed behind him, locking the door and heading toward my car across campus. I was rushing and not paying much attention to the people around me. The students passing by on their way to the library, cafeteria, and some even in their workout gear headed to the recreation center were basically a blur. Then my eyes landed on someone across from me. Her physique was familiar, the way she walked even stood out. But the woman I was staring at had on a pair of sweatpants and an oversized sweater. She was carrying a bag on her shoulder that read, "Ballet Life."

Ballet Life? Couldn't be her. I hurried my steps and caught up with the woman without getting too close. I caught a glimpse of her beautiful face as she turned to look both ways before crossing the street, and before she did, I yelled, "Morgan." She stilled and turned her head, searching the people around her.

Our conversations since that talk on Christmas were basic, at best. I'd text each day, a couple of times a day, to check in. Her responses didn't vary much, but at least I knew she was okay. Some days, she even told me she was great. Then after asking how I was, that would be the end of our conversation. We didn't get into what else she was doing, and if that involved a ballet class of some sort. But as I approached I got excited, thinking that maybe, just maybe, she found her passion again.

"Hey," I said as I stepped in closer to her, "What are you doing on campus?"

A warm smile spread across her face as she told me, "I'm going to dance class." My heart fluttered, mostly because of the smile she was wearing, but it helped that she was reconnecting with dance.

"I don't think I've seen you this happy since…" I considered our interactions since the fall and finally admitted, "Since we were walking this campus as students."

"Imagine that." Her eyes flickered, and I knew she must have had a painful memory. "I must admit, I'm glad I'm back dancing." I admired her face, the way her smile tugged at her lips, and her eyes glowed, the way her hair was pulled back on her head, how her shoulder peeked out from the neck of her sweatshirt. "I know you are a professor and all, but it feels like you are studying me right now." My eyes met hers, but her beautiful smile turned into a smirk.

"Could possibly be that you are the most beautiful woman I've ever met, and even more so now than when I saw you a few months ago." Her cheeks warmed, and her eyes blinked slowly. "I hope you continue choosing ballet, it looks good on you." I winked.

Her lip tucked between her teeth, and she told me, "I hope I keep choosing it," then she paused, "I just hope I keep choosing me. Above all else." Then her nose scrunched.

"Well, not above God, but everything else," she laughed slightly. "I want to continue rediscovering all the things I used to love, maybe even discovering new things to love."

She obviously was talking about hobbies, or whatever, but I couldn't help the goofy grin that ended up on my face when she said, "discovering new things to love." The thought of her loving me, as much as I was starting to realize I loved her, was remarkable.

"What is it that you used to love, outside of dance?" I craved the intricate details of her life. Getting to know what brought her joy. What would keep the smile on her face for a little while longer.

"The arts, creativity in different forms." She laughed and covered her mouth. "Ironically, I work at a law firm that uses little to no parts of my creativity." I frowned. "Have to pay the bills though, right?"

"Unfortunately." I nodded.

She looked down at her watch and I feared she was about to tell me she had to leave. That the interaction we had was coming to an end. When she said it though, I tapered my emotions so that it wouldn't deter her from what it was she was doing. "I should get going to class."

I told her, "Of course, have a good time," as she turned to walk away. As I continued the path to my car, I was in much less of a rush. The game that I was running home to watch wasn't even a concern anymore.

For a little more time with Morgan, I would have missed it all.

On the drive home, the only thing I could think about was her. Her smile reminded me of the kiss we shared, and that alone was enough to pray that God removed every hurt and pain that would prevent her from ever opening up again.

As I walked into my apartment, my phone rang, and I looked at the screen knowing that Matthew was ready to talk trash about the game. The game I should have been home to watch.

I hesitated before answering, trying to get the TV on first, at least. "Cody, man, did you see that shot?"

"I missed it," I told him, "Just walked into the house."

"Man, what?" he blurted. "Didn't you get off hours ago?"

"I did," I told him, "A student had a question—"

"Should have told them to read the notes."

I laughed. Of all the people I knew, Matthew was the least considerate when it came to students. Telling me different ways I should respond when they start asking too many questions, or don't do well on their tests. He tried to convince me that's how it was when we were in school, but even if I did remember that I wasn't trying to replicate it. "Then I ran into Morgan."

"Oh, for real?" he said, sounding much more interested in that than my experience with my student. "And what did the future Mrs. Felix have to say?"

He was convinced that Morgan was the one for me, still from the little time he saw the two of us together at homecoming. "I don't know about all that." I wasn't sure what would come of the two of us, and considering we weren't even dating anymore, going from nothing to married felt like a huge leap.

"So, what'd she say then?"

"She was on campus for a class. She's taking ballet."

"Oh, and she's lean, and flexible too." He laughed into the phone. "I mean, c'mon man, she sounds perfect."

I didn't tell Matthew about the problems Morgan was facing. The past she had with Elijah. He knew Elijah was a thing, that she had recently broken up with him, and that for whatever reason I wasn't a fan of his. At all. But he didn't know all the details. He didn't realize how many hurdles Morgan had to overcome.

"We'll see what happens, when it happens."

"Meanwhile, what other women are you out here trying to get with?"

"None," I said quickly. That was met with all types of mumbles and groans. "For real, I'm not really interested in getting to know someone else right now."

"So, what, you'll just wait around for Ms. Morgan? Hope one day she'll give you an honest chance?" He laughed. "That sounds crazy, man."

That wasn't as crazy as how I felt. That I'd wait for however long it took for her to be ready. "Guess they say love is crazy."

"Whoa." The one-word response let me know my thoughts weren't just in my head anymore, and that I had spoken them out loud. If I knew anything about Matthew, he wasn't going to let me live them down either. "Did you just say," he coughed, "The letters won't even form in my mouth. Unless you are my mama, the one and only woman who has ever heard me utter those words, I don't think I'll be able to even repeat what you just said." He went on, "About a woman you haven't even legit dated. A woman you've been tripping over for a decade, but still haven't even kissed." I let him keep believing that, explaining that we had kissed would lead to the what, when, where, and how. And as grown as I was, I didn't want to explain the situation that led up to it. "But here you are saying you, L," his mouth stopped short of saying the word, "her. I hope this all works out in the end. I need to be standing behind you at that altar when you recite your vows to her." Then he teased, "Wait, don't tell me you've already written them. Are they tucked away under your pillow, in your sock drawer or something?"

"Guess I'm about to go watch this game," I said, letting him know I was done with his tirade. "Later, man." I hung up before he could get in any more jokes.

Just when I thought talking to Matthew would have had my mind drifting from the kiss with Morgan, that's where my mind was as I sat in front of the TV and tried hard to watch the game.

Chapter Twenty-One

MORGAN

Ten weeks of dance. When I started the class, I didn't know if I still had what it would take to make it through one night of practice. But I did, and as the weeks went on, class after class, night after night, I only improved. Not only was I impressed by what my body could still do, I was intrigued by the young women in the class who were doing what I could do and more. So, when the instructor asked if I wanted to perform in the end-of-semester show, I was hesitant. I told her, "You sure? These girls will chew me up and spit me out."

She looked at me confidently and said, "And yet here you are."

I agreed to perform and was beyond excited for the show. I spent every spare hour I had practicing in the class with the other performers, and at home in the kitchen, bedroom, bathroom. Wherever I could. Even as I waited for papers at the copy machine, or had a spare minute between meetings, I was stretching and practicing positions. I slipped up and told Ava I was performing, and she promised she'd be in attendance.

I didn't expect anyone to be there. The show was more for me than anything else. I wanted to prove to myself that I could learn the routine and execute on stage. But it was nice for Ava to come into town just to be at the performance. I wondered who else would be in the audience and imagined it would mainly be A&T students, maybe their friends and family, potentially faculty. *Faculty. A&T Faculty.* Of course, that included Cody, but he was the last person I expected to be in the audience of the show. I didn't tell him about it, and I doubted he heard about it otherwise. At least that's what I told myself backstage as I tried to calm my nerves. The last thing I needed was a tumbling stomach while I was trying to maintain a perfect pointe.

I was mid-breath when I heard the instructor yell, "Five minutes, ladies."

My hands were shaking, and my heart was thumping. None of the techniques I used years prior were working—breathing deeply, imagining an emptied crowd, flexing each muscle of my body. Nothing. I was a few minutes from going on stage with adrenaline racing through my blood, feeling like I was on the verge of a heart attack. It was possible. After all, I was in my thirties and not my teens or young twenties anymore. I gripped at my chest and hoped, prayed, that wasn't the end of me.

How serendipitous that would have been. To finally make it back to the stage only to collapse of a heart attack and die.

Okay, maybe I was more than a little nervous, I was reeling. The anxious thoughts were just rushing me all at once, then I heard, "We're ready." I opened my eyes that had somehow sealed themselves shut during my tirade and saw everyone in their position in front of the stage entrance. I took a deep breath and squeezed myself into my spot. Second to walk onto the stage.

I questioned being front and center of the show, telling the instructor I could have easily fallen back. Just in case I needed to lean on those in front of me to remember the transitions, the count. She laughed and shook her head. Telling me, "Ms. Moore, you got this." As she gently rubbed a hand along my arm. There wasn't an "and if not" that followed. She trusted and believed that I would go on that stage and dance my butt off. And if she believed in me like that, how could I not?

The music started, and it seemed that my nerves melted away. The audience was a haze against the bright lights and that helped tremendously. I found myself lost within the ebbs and flows of the melody, flowing along as the tune hit the crescendo.

It was like the stage became a room in my house, and I was dancing in private, with no audience looking on. I was in my element.

At the end, the jeté that I perfectly landed on one leg was met with an outburst from the crowd, and it was then that I remembered I was performing in front of a packed auditorium.

"I knew you'd blow me away," the instructor whispered in my ear after wrapping me in a hug backstage. "That was beautiful, and the perfect way to end the show. I hope you'll be back next semester."

"Next semester," I repeated. "I think I might."

I knew Ava was in the audience waiting, so I pulled on a sweater to find her amongst the people in the crowd. When I saw her standing next to a woman, I assumed Ava was being overly kind and met a friend. Until the woman turned, and her face looked so like mine it made my mouth drop. "Mia," I screamed as I ran toward the two of them, "What are you doing here?" I asked, throwing my arms around her.

She laughed and pulled back, handing me a bouquet of flowers I didn't even notice she was holding. "Well, because my sister didn't tell me she was making a comeback to the stage, her bestie called and told me to hop a flight and see for myself." I looked at Ava with a mean side-eye and she shrugged. "That was perfect." Mia was beaming from ear to ear.

"Was it?" I asked.

Ava blurted, "It was, and I'm glad I made Mia get on that flight." They exchanged a glance then she said, "You deserve to have family here to watch you." I nodded and took a breath to keep the tear from falling. "Now we are headed to dinner to celebrate the prettiest ballerina on stage."

I laughed, thinking how she referenced me. "You act like we were all five," I mocked before I felt warmth on my back. I turned slowly. "Cody?"

Again, a bouquet of flowers was outstretched toward me, and behind the bouquet there was a smiling Cody. "Morgan," he said with his deeply calming voice, "That was amazing."

Leading up to the show I didn't expect anyone to be there, but to know Ava, Mia, and even Cody was in the audience, I felt overwhelmed. The tears released, but unlike many times before I wasn't hurting inside. I was bursting with joy.

The smile that wouldn't disappear made that clear. Cody swiped his thumb across my face. "Thank you for coming," I said as I leaned into the palm of his hand before backing away slightly.

"I wouldn't have missed this for the world. As soon as I heard the date announced I asked around to find out if you'd be performing."

"You did?"

"I did."

Behind me I could hear my sister and Ava whispering. I moved aside and said, "Cody, this is Mia, my sister."

His eyes opened wide, and he looked between the two of us before saying, "The resemblance is unbelievable." He reached his hand out to her and I watched as Mia experienced the Cody effect, her cheeks warming as she shook his hand and stared into his eyes.

I cleared my throat. "Thanks again for these flowers." I joked, "They are beautiful, but I still think the wilting lotus was my favorite." Before I let the memory of that day sink in, I said, "Really, I appreciate you being here."

"I've always imagined what you'd look like dancing on stage," he said softly. "It was better than anything I imagined. You were amazingly beautiful, and graceful. Your presence was captivating." It was me standing there with warm cheeks and a fire rushing through my blood.

"Wasn't she?" Ava blurted, causing me to break my stare with Cody's lips.

He looked to Ava, then to Mia, and said, "I'm sure you are about to celebrate your return to the stage, I won't keep you." He winked and turned to walk away.

"First of all, my God," was the first thing I heard from

Mia's mouth. "I think we have a lot to discuss. Let's get out of here."

After pulling on a different outfit, we left the auditorium and drove over to a nearby restaurant.

Inside, we raised our glasses and Ava said, "To the one person who I want more than anything to reignite her light." She beamed and we clanked our glasses together.

"Tonight was that for me," I told them both. "There is just something about getting lost in the music, flexing and bending my body gracefully. It was everything I knew I was missing all those years."

"Graceful," Mia sucked her teeth, "That's what he said too." She tilted her head to the side and said, "So I know Mr. Elijah is out of the picture, but I had no idea he was replaced with…" She fanned herself. "Might I dare say the sexiest chocolate man I've ever laid eyes on."

I laughed and reminded her that she had a man of her own at home. "And how would he feel about him not being the sexiest?"

She shrugged. "Sounds like a him problem." We all laughed. "But honestly, I need to know what is up with Mr. Man, and why the two of you aren't driving into the sunset together, hand in hand." She rested her chin on her palm and waited for me to respond.

I looked at Ava, a little panicked because I wasn't expecting to ever tell my sister about Elijah. I just hoped over time she'd forget about him, we'd move on, and I never would have to explain how terribly things ended. Mia had been in Elijah's presence plenty of times, and it was like around her he was on his best behavior. Manipulating her feelings for him, and in her eyes, he could do no wrong.

Even when I briefly told her we had broken up, she told

me she'd be praying we'd work through it. Saying, "He's going to be my brother-in-law one day, I just know it." At the time, I was too stuck in the pain to drag her into it with me. I knew telling her the truth about him would remind her of our mom and how we endured watching her night after night, be beaten and verbally abused.

"Is there something I'm missing?" Mia looked at Ava with pleading eyes, but Ava turned her glance to me. "Morgan, what is it?"

"I don't know where to start." Explaining that me and Cody couldn't ride off into the sunset because I needed to love myself again felt misleading.

"How about from the beginning." Ava reached over and placed a hand over mine. "She'll understand." Ava's voice was reassuring.

So, I started from the beginning. "Elijah and I broke up because he hit me." I winced like a Band-Aid had been ripped from my arm, taking with it all the thin hairs beneath it.

And like I had slapped her, Mia gasped. "No, he didn't." I could see her face growing red, even through her caramel complexion. "I'll kill him." She blurted, then whispered, "Or have someone to do it for me. I'm not cut out for a jail cell, but that man right there deserves what's coming for him." She reached for her phone, and I wondered who exactly she was going to call.

Ava reached for her hand, calming both of us, she said, "Just listen, Mia."

"It didn't start with that. Over the last couple of years he had grown increasingly less tolerable. Talking to me any type of way, breaking my confidence, making me feel like my world should revolve around him when I wasn't even close to being a blip in his. He made me isolate from my friends, and even you guys. It was like if it wasn't him, it couldn't be anyone else. I prayed so hard for God to change him, and when he didn't, I backed away from Him too." I took a deep breath. "I never shared with you because I didn't want you to be reminded of Mama." I closed my eyes and took a deep breath. The truth I revealed gutted me. I was more winded than when I was on stage, clutching for air to fill my lungs again.

"Oh, Morgan." She stood from her seat and wrapped her arms around me. "You should have told me." She snickered, "Had me over here praying the two of you would get back together when I should have been praying he tripped and fell into a ditch." I smacked her arm, and she took her seat. "But seriously though, I'm sorry you endured any of that." Her eyes fluttered shut. "Not in a million years would I have wished what we watched with Mama on either of us."

"For many years, I vowed I'd never be in a relationship like hers, and that's exactly what I ended up with. It's like a cruel joke." I shook my head. "At first, some parts of me rationalized with it, that it wasn't as bad as what Mama went through so I could stick beside him." I assured her, "But when the words weren't enough and he hit me, I knew I had to end it."

For the first time, I was able to talk about Elijah without crying. But I heard a sniffle and turned to see Ava wiping a tear away. "Ava," I whispered, "Please don't cry." I reminded her, "Don't let him steal tonight from us, we are supposed to be celebrating."

"That's right. We are," Mia announced. "Tonight, we are celebrating the end of a decade-long drama, and the start of something even more beautiful." She looked at me cautiously before asking, "So, Chocolate Man of the Year? You are keeping him at arm's length because of your ex?"

I wagged my head. "I met him freshman year of college. He moved away, then recently returned. He's teaching on campus." It wasn't exactly an answer to her question, but at least it gave her an idea of how the two of us knew each other.

"Look at that." She smiled. "He seems caring, thoughtful. And did we already establish he's sexy?" I laughed. "What?" She shrugged. "I'm just saying." Then her smile faded, and she asked, "How does he treat you?"

"Months ago we went out, and things were going well, but I had to slow it down. I'm not ready," I told her, "But even though we haven't been out in months, he texts or calls and checks on me every day."

"Every day?" Mia's eyes were wide, and Ava tilted her head to the side. "I understand that getting over what the man who is not worthy of me speaking his name put you through had to be hell. And I know it'll take time before you are ready to open again. It's sad that Mama engrained in us that we should accept what little good was offered to us while we overlooked the bad. And it's taken me a ton of couch time to realize I deserve better than just *kinda good*." She reached her hand out and placed it over mine. "Maybe that'll be helpful for you too." She grinned as she added, "Because have you considered that God is bringing the two of you together, in like a full circle moment? That maybe him being here, now, isn't just a coincidence?"

I had to bite the side of my lip to hide the smile that wanted to erupt. "He calls it God's handiwork."

Ava asked, "What's that?"

"He doesn't believe in coincidences, just that God is orchestrating things on our behalf."

"That," Ava said, pointing to me, "That's it. You know what to look out for now. And we already agreed I'm going to call flag on the play if I ever see anything that is not right."

"And," Mia interrupted, "Might I add, I can help you find a therapist who will help you build up your trust reservoir. I was told mine had been depleted, and that's just from what I saw with Mama." She cocked her head to the side. "Don't let that man ruin what could be great for you."

I looked between the two of them and said, "You know, somehow I think if it was me and Cody in college, I would have been in a much better position now."

The thought of everything that could have been had I not stayed with Elijah for so long taunted me. That maybe if I would have dated someone else, someone kind, someone patient, someone compassionate, someone like Cody, that maybe I would have even pursued my wildest dreams.

Ava said, "Well buttercup, there's no room for regret. And that includes now. You'd hate to look back on this point and regret what could have been." She stretched her arms and said, "But I think it's time for us to get back into celebration mode. I'm hungry," she said with a scowl as she rubbed her belly.

Finally, back at home, after hours of eating and talking with Mia and Ava at the restaurant, I left them in the living room so I could send a necessary text.

Morgan: Thank you again for the flowers, and more so for your presence.
Morgan: Thank you for just being you, kind, compassionate, and caring.

Before I bombarded his phone with messages at

midnight, I sat my phone on the bed beside me, closed my eyes, and started a prayer. "God, thank you for the ability to dance tonight, for returning me to my passion. Thank you for allowing Ava and Mia to be here with me." I was prepared to say Amen and call it a night, but I added, "God, thank you for Cody. If this is your handiwork, allow me to be open to receiving everything you have for me. Amen."

Chapter Twenty-Two

CODY

Since seeing Morgan at her performance, and the text message she sent after, she and I were talking much more often and for longer. We'd stay up on the phone until she'd fall asleep, and she was the first voice I listened to when I woke up in the morning.

Still, she wasn't exactly telling me she was ready for anything more. So, when I heard about the art exhibit at the museum, I told her I'd be going, but hesitated and decided not to ask her to join me. I still wanted to give her the space she needed if she still needed it.

Walking into the museum, I immediately wished she was there with me. There were amazing pieces that I would have loved to talk to her about, especially the one that was labeled "Art in motion." I stood in front of it, looking at the intricate details of the painting, focusing in on each element of it before standing back and re-evaluating it with a larger focus on the entire canvas.

"This is amazing, isn't it?" I heard someone ask beside me.

I looked to my right at the gorgeous woman standing there, a woman I'd seen a few times on campus. "It is. I don't even know how his mind created this vision." Of course, I was nowhere near a creative, I enjoyed art from the sidelines. Not contributing in any way to the forum. But I could appreciate the intricacies of it. "The individual brushes feel like the image is moving, right?"

I turned from her and looked at the painting again but could feel the woman's stare on the side of my face. "Definitely. And I heard that it took him years to finish it." She laughed softly. "Imagine working on something for years, the patience…"

"But the beauty that presented itself after the wait." I wiped a hand across my beard. "I'm sure he'd tell us all it was well worth it."

"I'm sure." She took a sip of the champagne in her hand before she asked, "How are you liking being back on campus?" Although I encountered her on different occasions, we never did more than pass pleasantries. I never told her about returning to A&T, or that I was an alum.

"I'm enjoying it," I said apprehensively.

She laughed and placed a hand on my arm. "When you are as *interesting* as you are, people talk."

I looked down at her hand, then back up to her. "I see." My eyes didn't stay on hers though, there was someone behind her that caught my attention. As I watched her glide through the room, her dress flowing behind her, I was captivated. Like the painting in front of me, she was a work of art.

Morgan's eyes found mine, then I saw her tense and look away. Not what I expected considering it'd been a while since we'd seen each other. My natural reaction was to go toward her, but hers was to flee away from me. "A friend just walked in," I told the teacher as she slid her hand from my arm, "It was nice talking with you."

I walked away in search of Morgan and found her standing in front of a sculpture of a man. "Morgan," I said softly, and she turned toward me. "I promise running into you feels like a gift I never want to lose," I said with a smile. But the look she gave me was strained. As if she wanted to smile, she wanted to be happy, but for some reason couldn't.

"I've been naive," she started, and I just listened. "I've been talking to you all this time, but not until tonight did I consider you may be dating someone." Before I could interrupt, she rambled, "Not that there would be anything wrong with that, because you are an amazing guy and deserve to be happy. To be with someone who can accept and reciprocate your love. I just thought—"

"I don't understand." I shook my head, trying to think of what I may have missed between our last conversation and that moment.

"The woman," she looked behind me, "that you were just with, she's gorgeous."

"Didn't think I'd ever see a *jealous* Morgan," I snickered, but she scowled. "But I'm tempted to tell you that woman is my girlfriend just to see that look in your eyes a little longer."

Her eyes narrowed, and her mouth opened slightly. "She's not?"

"I'm very single." Although, with a single word, I would have gladly changed that status for her. "Have you eaten?"

"Not yet," she told me, "I was going to look around then head home and find something to munch on."

"Mind if we do one or both of those together?"

"I'd like to do both." She winked.

I pointed at the path and told her, "Lead the way." I didn't tell her I'd follow her to the end of the earth and back if she asked me to, but I would have. There was something about Morgan that I was drawn to. It wasn't just her beauty, because if it was that the teacher would have had my allegiance. It was her, the woman that despite all her mess, was still kind, and generous, and if given the opportunity, I was sure she would be an immensely passionate lover. I could only imagine her love for her partner being like it was for dance—deeply rooted and inspiring.

"This is creative," she said as we stood in front of an abstract piece of art, tilting her head to both sides, "I'm not sure where to focus my eyes."

With one look I told her, "There isn't a singular focus, its complexities make it uniquely beautiful." I looked to her and said, "It reminds me of you."

The tug of her lip between her teeth had me feeling like I could have found a dark room and pulled her inside of it with me. Instead, I shifted my legs and turned my attention to the art. "If you had one focal area, where would it be?"

"My heart," she offered easily, "Definitely my heart." Then she uttered, "And I'd imagine it looks a little like this picture…" She turned to me, and I faced her. "Complex."

"Unlike this piece of art, in its final state, I hope there is still room for your heart to change. To simplify."

"I think so."

We continued around the exhibit until she announced, "Somehow, looking at all this art has made me very hungry."

Before she could suggest we leave, I said, "Guess we better feed you then. I'll drive?"

Sitting across from Morgan in the restaurant felt right. It didn't feel like it'd been months since the last time we enjoyed a meal together. Or that the majority of our conversations were over the phone, or text. We naturally slid into a conversation that made me want the night to extend on to forever.

"This was good, thank you." She looked at me cautiously before she added, "Tonight, as unplanned as it was, turned out to be pretty amazing."

"I think so too."

"Can I ask you something?" I nodded. "Why didn't you invite me out? You told me about the exhibit but didn't extend an invitation."

I smirked. "I wasn't sure if you were ready to go out again, honestly." Then I told her, "Remember freshman year?"

She shrugged. "A lot of it."

"We spent a lot of time together in the library, coffee shop, or what not." She nodded along with me. "There were so many times back then when I wanted to ask you out."

Her eyes widened. "Why didn't you?"

"It just never felt like the right time." I didn't mention her ex, and the fact that he quickly became a permanent fixture in her life. "Then it was apparent that you were obviously taken. Over time, I figured you weren't the one for me." She looked down at her lap. "Then seeing you again, I thought maybe you were for me, and it just wasn't the right time." I cleared my throat. "It still might not be the right time, but I'm willing to wait until it is."

A tear slipped down her face, and that was the last thing I wanted to see. "I've seen you cry rivers, Morgan." I reached across the table and wiped the tear away. "The last thing I want to do is to add to that endless stream, unless," I smiled, "they are tears of joy."

She smiled. "I think this time, they are." Then she said, "What you just shared, it's the sweetest thing you could have ever said to me." She took a deep breath, closed her eyes, and when she re-opened them she asked, "But, how long will be too long to wait?"

With a smirk, I told her, "It's already been over a decade, and yet here I am."

"Here you are," she repeated.

What came next was unexpected but welcomed. "I started talking to a therapist recently. Trying to work through some of my *stuff*." I watched as her chest heaved. "It's helping. Sometimes I wish she could just snap her finger and fix me." She snapped her finger almost as if it would happen. "But I know it'll take time."

I leaned in and reached for her hand, and when I felt the smoothness of her palm I said, "Imagine if a worm tried to bust out of a cocoon before it was time." She had a puzzled look on her face. "It'd miss out on the beauty of becoming a butterfly."

A small smile crept up on her face. "I never knew you waxed so poetically." Her laughter filled the table and the space around us. The joy on her face made my chest swell, and well, something else too. I adjusted in my seat and focused on the fork in front of me.

Knowing our plates were cleaned, I hoped she would agree when I asked, "Would you like dessert?"

"If I didn't know better, Cody, I'd think you were trying to stay here all night." She looked beside us at the clearing tables. "Feels like we may be closing the place out."

"Your suspicion may be right." I smiled. "I have been hesitating all night." She looked at me as her eyes narrowed. "I wanted to know if you would like to join me on vacation. I'll be off for the summer and wanted to take a quick trip at the beginning. I'd love for you to come along."

Her facial expression didn't change, she barely even blinked, but as I watched her chest heaving, I wondered if she was considering saying, "Yes."

Chapter Twenty-Three

MORGAN

"I don't think I'm ready for it though," I said cautiously as I stared out the window of the therapist's office. As she always did, she stared at me and allowed me to think through what it was I needed to say or to talk my feelings out loud. When I first started therapy, she told me sometimes people just needed a sounding board, but everything we needed to know, all the answers we were seeking, were already inside of us. "In all the years I spent with Elijah we never took a vacation together. And for Cody to ask me when we aren't even dating, it feels…" I shrugged. "I don't even know what it feels like."

She quietly offered, "Overwhelming? Fearful? Like you don't deserve to go on vacation with a man who seemingly feels…" I turned from the window to watch the words as they left her mouth. "Right?" I nodded. "From what you've shared about Cody, he doesn't seem like he is forcing anything you aren't ready for. So, if you decide you do not want to take this vacation," she held a finger in the air, "I don't think it'll upset him if you were to decline his offer." Her finger danced. "But, if the only reason you are declining his offer is because you've never done it before, then I think you should sit with those thoughts for a while and see what's at the root of it."

After a moment, I said randomly, "All this time I felt like I couldn't trust someone else with my heart, but now, after our sessions, I'm starting to realize it's me I can't trust with my heart."

She looked at me with a soft smile. "That's something we should explore." I knew our session was over and she was about to tell me what work I'd need to do on my own, at home, so I listened with intention. "I want you to think of all the ways you feel you've failed yourself. Then think of what was involved, who was involved, and when we meet again we will discuss what you've discovered."

The drive home was long, and instead of sitting with the thoughts I had, I wanted to talk to someone else. About anything, and everything. I didn't want the silence haunting me all the way home. So, I called Ava and she answered after a couple of rings. "What's up buttercup," then she paused, "Leaving Dr. Freeman's office?"

"Yes," I sighed. It was typical for me to call Ava after my session. I'd go into such heavy feelings with Dr. Freeman, I just needed something light. Ava never hesitated to make me laugh.

"You know," she started, "I'm so proud of you for doing the work." She told me, "It's so encouraging to see that you realized you had some baggage you needed to unload before stepping into another situation and collecting more. So many people just continue carrying the weight." Her words weren't giving what I hoped they would give, and I wondered what it was weighing on her mind.

"What's going on, Ava?"

Her breathing and shuffling were the only indication that our call was still connected. Then finally she admitted, "Just these guys I've been on dates with lately all seem to be dealing with ex issues, and projecting whatever they experienced with them, onto me." I heard a loud clap. "And I'm not them." Then she huffed, "But that's a conversation for another day."

I laughed. "Oh Ava, who would have thought finding love would be this difficult?" I joked, "Think there is a monastery with two open beds that'll take us?"

She scoffed. "Speak for yourself girl, even with ex issues, mama issues, or whatever, I can't give up the…"

I blurted, "Ava," then told her, "I get it though. It would be hard." That made me think of the last time I had even had sex. It'd been the longest period, since, well, ever. "You know what," I told her, "I think it's been almost a year since the last time I've had sex." The gasp that exited her mouth startled me, and I jumped, jerking the wheel to the right. "Shoot," I mumbled under my breath as I looked out the passenger window to make sure the person beside me was good.

"A year, Morgan? My God."

"I feel like I shouldn't even think about it, or I'll awake a sleeping giant." I laughed, thinking it was already too late.

"So, Cody hasn't tried to rub up on your booty yet?"

I considered the one time I hopped into his lap, and how he stopped my agenda before it could proceed too far. Or the night at the museum, the extended dinner that followed, the car ride back, and the lingering stares he gave me but only offered me a comforting hug and a kiss to my cheek before walking away. "No. He hasn't."

I could sense her judging and knew whatever she said next was not likely to be favorable toward Cody. "That's commendable. Because clearly he is very attracted to you."

"I…" As I pulled into my parking spot and turned off my car, I told her, "I didn't think you were going to say that." I looked up at my steps, then over my shoulder before exiting the car. "I thought you were going to drag him for not coming on to me."

"For what?" She told me, "That man has been beyond reproach. Seems like an amazing guy, and to be honest, I wish I could find a man like him." She laughed, "Now, would I like to know if that man can have both kindness and superpowers in the bed, yes. Of course. But I just imagine he'd be as mindful of your body as he's been with your heart."

I opened the door to my house, and I felt every word she said. "You know, Ava, you're right. I think you just helped me come to a conclusion about this trip."

She clapped her hands and yelled, "Please tell me you are going."

"I think I might," I told her as my face hurt from the wide smile it was rocking.

I'd been warned that road trips with men could be devastatingly brutal. That guys were always about the destination and didn't want to stop along the way. Still, I hopped in the passenger seat of Cody's rental happily. Three and a half hours in the car with him felt like no time at all. Although we only stopped once, I didn't mind our extended conversations, and pointing out different landmarks as we drove down the highway.

When we pulled up to the hotel, I stopped talking and just stared ahead. "You okay?" Cody asked.

"Yeah," I said softly. I didn't plan on sharing anything about Elijah with him but felt it may shape some of the emotions he could witness me battling. "Me and Elijah never took a trip together. Outside of visiting his parents for holidays, we never vacationed together." I bit the side of my mouth.

"Oh." His mouth hung open and he wiped a hand across his face. "I wish I would have known that." He cringed. "I would have picked somewhere better than Myrtle Beach for your first," he hesitated, "trip with a guy."

I laughed. "That was real *formal*." He shrugged. "I know, kinda hard to explain this, right?" He nodded. "But whatever this is, I'm happy to be anywhere with you." There was a look of surprise in his eyes. "In fact, I would have taken a tent in the woods, and it still would have been a great time."

He leaned over the console and placed a soft kiss on my cheek. "That's sweet, but I'm not a fan of mosquitos." We both laughed. "Ready to start this vacation?"

I nodded excitedly as he hopped out of the car and opened my door. Our luggage wheeling behind us, we walked into the lobby of the luxurious hotel. Although we were in Myrtle Beach, I could imagine the hotel being anywhere else in the world. The decor and smiling staff were welcoming. As we made it to the front desk, and Cody started checking in, I heard the woman tell him, "I have a king-size bed suite for you with a beautiful ocean view."

Cody was smiling and nodding, and I felt my heart racing. Leading up to the trip, we didn't talk about what the trip would mean for us. As much as we talked about the excursions and sight-seeing we could do, we didn't discuss what would happen in the room. "Alright, Mr. Felix, you're all set. Two keys, and the elevators are to the right."

As Cody turned to walk toward the elevators I couldn't move. My legs were stuck as I stared at his retreating back. Months ago, I was crawling into his lap and would have jumped at an opportunity to be with him in a king-sized bed overlooking the ocean.

Somehow, I went from that to being terrified at the possibility.

"Morgan?" His deep, calming voice relaxed me slightly and I watched as he approached me. "Are you okay?"

"Yes." I forced a smile. "I'm great. Ready?" He narrowed his eyes then nodded his head.

The elevator ride up, Cody was talking about lunch and which of the hotel's three restaurants we could try first, but I was counting silently in my head the moments until the elevator doors opened.

When they did, I let him lead the way. Following behind him, aware of each step I took. Then the door of the room opened, and he stood aside letting me take the first look. "It's beautiful," I said, moving past the bed and to the window to the balcony set up with chairs. I cracked the door open to listen to the crashing waves. "So serene," I told him.

He stood beside me. "It is. Something about the ocean has such a calming effect, right?" I nodded. "We'll have time to enjoy this view later. I'm a little hungry. Want to head down?"

"Yes," I told him, glad to be leaving the room.

"It's nice outside, would you like to eat on the patio?" he asked as we stood at the hostess stand.

"That'll be nice," I said.

The patio was casual—families with children running past, the view of the ocean, birds taking flight—my heart was calm, and my hands settled on my lap finally. "How do you feel about jet skiing?" Cody asked after the waitress took our order.

I looked out to the ocean and felt it was the best time to let him know, "I can't swim."

"If it'll make you comfortable, you'll have on a life jacket, and I promise I won't let anything happen to you."

I tilted my head to the side and stared at him for a minute, before I said, "Can I trust you to help me if we are in the middle of the ocean though?"

He laughed. "Let's hope that doesn't happen. But yes, you can trust me. I hope you can trust me on land, sea, or in the air."

I can trust you. But whether I trust me is still questionable. "Strangely, I do."

He tilted his head to the side and asked again, "So, jet skiing?"

"Jet skiing."

Although I watched the people on the jet skis and small boats right off the shore, I wasn't so sure I wanted to be one of those people in the middle of the ocean hardly recognizable by anyone on the beach. "That's a lot of water," I said as I took a small bite of my sandwich.

Cody was trying his hardest not to laugh. "What's the most adventurous thing you've ever done?"

I thought long and hard before I replied, "You know that free-fall ride," I put my hand above my head, "That just drops out of the sky." His eyes widened as my hand fell beside me quickly. "Not me." I laughed. "Let's see." By the time I told him, "I guess I'm not all that adventurous," he was buckled over in laughter. Wiping tears from his eyes as he sniffled.

"Alright, that's fair, but you leap through the air, trusting the ground will absorb your weight when you fall."

I jerked my head back and placed a hand on my chest. "Are you saying I'm…" I lowered my voice, "heavy?" He was laughing again, and I wasn't a comedian but suddenly I wanted to do improv. Anything to keep him laughing just like that. "Is it sad that I haven't witnessed you laugh often?"

We both grew silent at the realization. "You must have thought I was walking around with a stick up my butt." I wagged my head. "Really?" He laughed again, and whatever had gotten into him, I didn't want it to leave.

"I like seeing you balled over in a fit of laughter." My lip curled up. "It's attractive."

"Is it now?" But the laughing had stopped, and his face transformed into the serious side I'd been used to seeing. Except his eyes, the way he looked at me was like he was a predator, and I had become his prey. I gulped and grabbed the drink from the table, sipping it down quickly to calm my heated body.

"Wow," I said, shifting in the seat and glancing back to the water. "Think the ocean is cold?" I hoped so, because I needed something to chill me all the way out.

"Won't know till we dip our toes in." I looked down at the sundress I wore for the road trip and remembered to get in the water, I'd need to change into my bathing suit.

"Oh," I told him, "We should probably change." He nodded and called the waiter over to settle the bill.

"I can't wait to see you in the water."

I looked at him and could only imagine what he really

meant to say was that he couldn't wait to see me half-naked. At least that's what I was thinking as I looked at him. "Just remember your promise. You'll save me even if that means I have to crawl on top of your head to get back onto the jet ski."

He clutched his chest. "When you put it like that…" His eyes widened.

I grabbed his arm and told him, "I wouldn't do you like that. Just tell my family and Ava I love them," I joked.

Inside the room, he offered, "You can change first."

Shuffling through my suitcase, I found one of the bathing suits I bought before we left. It was a bright pink two-piece that covered just enough of my body, but not too much. Trying it on in the store, it felt right. Knowing I was about to be wearing it in front of Cody, after he'd given me that look, was a little different.

Still, I hurried to the bathroom and changed into it. Posing in the mirror, looking at myself from different angles, until I was satisfied with what I saw.

I stepped out of the bathroom, expecting that Cody would be headed in when I saw his bare, broad back in front of the window. "Oh," I said, and as he turned my eyes fell to his torso. *Oh.* My mouth was likely hanging open as I couldn't tear my eyes away from the muscles formed in his stomach. "Looks like you are ready." But I wouldn't know if he still had on the shorts from the trip or not, because my eyes still wouldn't leave his well-formed abs.

He walked closer to me and reached for my hand, asking, "You good, Morgan?" in a tone that was lower than usual. It rumbled out of his mouth like a lion, and I felt like an antelope caught in his path.

Finally, I inched my eyes up to meet his and said, "Yes," with wide eyes. "I'm good. You good?"

I felt his hand on my chin, and he said, "I'm better than good." A knot formed in my throat as I tried to gulp it down. His eyes scanned my body and he asked, "Did you put on sunscreen?" The reminder dousing me like a bucket of ice water.

"No," I told him, "I should though, right?" He nodded and his mouth formed but the words didn't come out. "I'll grab it." I moved to my bag and searched for the sunscreen, holding it up. "Here it is."

"Need help?" Our eyes connected and I knew all the fears I had about being in a room with him, sharing a bed, would resolve if I felt his hands on my skin. His warmth caressing me as he rubbed the sunscreen into every inch of my exposed skin.

I shook my head slightly and watched as a frown formed but quickly fell away from his face. "I think I got it." Twisting the cap off the bottle, I focused all my attention on the cream that poured from the bottle, carefully massaging it into my skin.

Then I turned to the side and saw Cody shift awkwardly. "I'm just going to go grab the beach towels." He pointed toward the front door. "I think I saw some over here."

Lathered up, I asked, "Did you need some?"

"Ugh, yeah," he said, looking at me as I stood closely behind him. "Mind helping me get my back?"

I shook my head. "No, I don't mind." I squeezed a blob into my hand, rubbed it between my hands, then massaged it slowly into his back. Admiring the curve of his shoulders and his deep-set muscles. "I didn't realize you worked out…" I strained as I reached the center of his back, nearing the waistband of his shorts, "often."

"Something like that," he said as a muscle flinched beneath my hands.

"Alright, I think we are both safe from the sun's rays." As if that was the only heat we'd need to be protected from. "Ready?"

He turned to me, towels in his hand, and said, "I'm ready." Thankfully, he opened the door and led us out, because the way his eyes looked at me when he said that, I wanted to pull him by the arms and onto the bed.

The entire walk to the beach, Cody tried to ease my nerves about taking on the expansive ocean. Telling me, "You'll be going so fast on the back of the jet ski you won't even notice you are out in the open sea."

"Speed. Fast. Great," I mumbled as we neared the water-sport section of the beach. I covered my brow with a hand and looked out into the ocean while Cody coordinated the rental with the guy.

"I'll drive," he said, and as I turned his way, "That is if you don't mind holding on."

"I don't mind." He opened a life jacket and I walked into as he tugged on the straps, making sure it was secure. "Thanks," I said as he stood close enough to block the sun from my eyes.

We eased our way into the cool water, and I waited for him to climb on the back before I hopped on. If I had never prayed a protection prayer before, I made sure to mouth one then. "God, keep us secure and safe from harm on this jet ski." I looked up to him and whispered, "Amen," as I climbed onto the jet ski, wrapped my arms around his waist, and leaned into his back.

"Make sure you hold on." He looked over his shoulder. "Okay?" His life jacket kept me from feeling the warmth of his back but holding on to his waist had me feeling secure. Secure enough to not notice the stream of water splashing in my face as he sped off into the ocean, away from the shore. I clenched my eyes closed as the people on the beach became tiny specks.

"Are you okay?" I heard him shout over the sound of the engine and the crashing of the jet ski against the waves. I peeked my eyes open long enough to see his face, before just nodding in response. It took a while, but before we were finished, I had relaxed and laughed as he crossed waves, causing us to bounce along the water. By the time we were pulling back up to shore I had a wide grin. "Look at that, safe and sound."

I felt the sand beneath my feet, between my toes, and said, "Thank God." Cody helped me out of my life jacket, then even adjusted the straps of my bathing suit before taking my hand and walking us toward a beach chair and umbrella.

"Feel like sitting out for a while?"

"Only if you don't mind me dozing off," I said with a weak smile. The long car ride, full stomach, and sun was the perfect setup for a mid-day nap.

"Whatever makes you comfortable," he said with ease as he positioned the umbrella to block most of the sun for both of us.

It was the best nap ever. But when I finally woke from a cool breeze, I realized the sun had set. I looked to my side and realized Cody had fallen asleep and was still sleep. I moved to his lounge chair and nudged his side. "Cody," I said softly.

Before he woke, his arm went to my leg, and my body

shivered. His eyes sprung open, and he mumbled, "Sorry," as he moved his hand and stretched his body. He laughed. "Guess you looked too comfortable over there, I couldn't let you be the only one enjoying an oceanfront nap."

"It was a good nap." I looked around at the almost emptied beach. "But we should probably get inside. It's a little cold." I rubbed my hands against my arms.

"You're right," he said.

I wrapped my towel around my body as we made our way back into the hotel. In the elevator, I suggested, "What do you think about room service tonight instead of getting dressed and going back out?"

"I think that's a good idea." He placed a fist over his mouth to cover a yawn. "The sun has drained me."

"Me too."

Inside the room, I opened my luggage and pulled out an oversized shirt. Nothing that screamed, *I want to share a bed with you.* "I'm going to hop in the shower."

Inside the bathroom, I looked in the mirror and imagined what it would be like to be with Cody. Not just sexually, but in a relationship. I imagined it'd be like the day we spent together—full of laughter, joy, and comfort.

Then I remembered the list that Dr. Freeman had me create, and the reasons I didn't trust myself, and I frowned. I needed the stream of the shower to release all the tension that had started to build up from the memory.

Walking from the bathroom, Cody stood before me and asked, "All done?" as he stood with clothes in his hand. His eyes gazing down before quickly meeting mine again.

"All done," I repeated as I wondered what type of clothes he planned to wear to bed.

While he was in the shower, the food arrived, and I set it

in front of the window while I waited for him to finish. He came out with a pair of shorts and a t-shirt, and I was thankful we both chose the modest route. "Let's eat." He rubbed his belly and licked his lips as he approached me, and my heart thumped, sending vibrations between my thighs.

As we ate, we casually talked about the day and the ideas he had for the rest of the weekend. It was easy, fun, gentle—the things that were so hard to come by toward the end of my relationship with Elijah. I enjoyed the simplicity of it all. I noted that as we finished our food. "This," I pointed to him, "Whatever we have, feels so easy."

"It does," he said before his eyes flicked to the bed. "But I've been avoiding the obvious all day." He cringed. "I don't think we are ready for—"

"By we," I asked, "do you actually mean me?" He nodded. "You're right." Then I quickly added, "Physically, I'm there. I'm all the way there," I told him with a lazy smile. "Mentally, emotionally…" I shook my head.

He reached his hand out and told me, "No pressure, ever." He plopped his free hand to the couch and said, "I'll take this." Then he noted, "Because when you are ready…" He stared at me for a beat. "I want to know there's no turning back."

My eyes widened before I leaned forward, our foreheads resting against each other's. My hand went to the side of his face, and I inhaled before I let my lips graze his softly, gently.

Chapter Twenty-Four

CODY

There wasn't anything special about turning thirty-two. It wasn't like ten, sixteen, eighteen, or twenty-one even. I wasn't expecting a lot to happen, no surprise parties or elaborate gifts from my family and friends. The few texts and phone calls that started early in the morning were the extent of what I anticipated for that day.

But by that afternoon, when I hadn't heard from Morgan I was thinking something was up.

I'd sent my usual good morning text, and it was left on read. The follow-up text asking if she wanted to join me for lunch did too. By that evening, when I just wanted to see her to end my night, and she didn't answer her phone, I started to panic.

What if Elijah came back, drunk and disorderly, and... I couldn't even think about the rest of that statement. Instead of waiting for her to answer, I drove to her house.

Her car wasn't outside, and the house was dark. I saw no signs of Elijah nearby, or the car he drove away the day I pulled up on the two of them. Just in case, I walked up to her front door and knocked.

While standing there, I dialed her number again. Just before I hung up, she answered. "Thank God," I mumbled. "Morgan, are you okay?" Her voice was faint, and I could hear her sniffling. "Morgan, what's wrong?"

"Cody, I'm so sorry," she started, and my heart did a flip. Felt like it was wrenching as I waited for her to continue. "Happy birthday."

"Thank you, but where are you? Are you okay? I'm standing in front of your house."

I heard her breath over the phone, then she told me, "I'm not there." I ran back down the stairs toward my car. "I had to fly to Florida."

"Florida?" Then I paused at my car door. "Your mom? Is she okay?"

It was like my words gave her tears permission to release and as they did, I held my head back, praying that whatever her mom was going through she would be okay. Morgan didn't talk about her mom often, and when she did it was only to share of the traumatizing incidents. Never anything loving or joyful, nothing like I shared with her about my mom.

But when she said, "She's in the hospital," my fist clenched beside me. "She'll probably be here for a few days." I heard her shuffle, then settle again before she said, "It was her boyfriend." She snickered. "Broke her rib, and her face," she sighed deeply, "it's bruised and battered."

"I'm sorry, Morgan." I knew that was hard for her. Not only seeing her mom in that state, but rehashing memories of

Elijah and everything she was trying to work through to move past that. "Is there anything I can do?" As she tried to tell me she'd be okay, I could hear her voice shaking.

"No, I just wish I didn't have to see her like this," she said quietly.

"Can you send me the address of the hospital?"

"Sure," she agreed absently. "She's waking up though, mind if I call you back in a bit?" I could hear her trying to smile. "I can at least sing you happy birthday."

"Of course," I told her.

As soon as I was off the phone with her I pulled up a travel website and looked for the next flight to… "Shoot, where is she?" I looked at my phone and was thankful when the address popped up in my text. "Tampa."

There was a flight leaving from Piedmont in three hours. I booked it and a hotel, and raced home to throw some clothes into a bag.

On my way to the airport, I called my mom, the one person I knew could pray like no other, and I knew she wouldn't hesitate to pray for Morgan's mom. "Hey Mom," I said when she answered.

"Birthday boy," she started, "Change your mind about coming by for me to make you dinner?" I could hear my dad in the background speaking, "We threw an extra steak on the grill just in case."

"Actually, I'm headed to the airport."

As she repeated, "Airport?" I heard my dad saying the same.

"It's Morgan's mom, she's in the hospital, and I just want to be there for Morgan."

"Oh, of course, baby. That's understandable." Then she

paused. "Is everything going to be okay?" I could hear the concern in her voice.

"Mama," my voice felt like it was about to shatter, "Could you just pray for her," I hesitated, "And Morgan."

"Of course, dear. Let's pray together." She started before I could even agree. "Heavenly Father, we are coming before you on behalf of Morgan's mother, and Morgan. Dear God, we know that you are a healer, and you can do the miraculous. Please put your hands on her mother, heal her, be with the doctors and the nurses so that they can treat her. And God, be with Morgan, heal her heart, ease her mind, and bring her peace during this time. God I know that you can, and that you will. Be with my baby as he travels to be with them, Lord. Protect him, and his peace. Allow him to be a light during this dark time. In Jesus's name we pray, Amen."

I cleared my throat and softly agreed, "Amen. Thank you Mama. I needed that."

"And I need you, so take care of yourself, okay?"

"Okay. I'll let you know when I land. I love you," I told her before getting off the phone.

The three-hour flight felt like it was an eternity plus a little more. By the time I landed, I was exhausted, but raced to the rental car counter to rent something. Anything.

I'd never been in Tampa, so navigating was a challenge, even with the GPS guiding me. But I finally made it to the hospital and called Morgan from the entrance.

"Hey." She sounded like she was sleep or in a deep space. "What room is your mom in?" I asked.

"In room 305. Hold on," she said, "Let me step out so I can sing." Her voice sounded a little more uplifted as she began, "Happy birthday to you," I wanted to hear her rendition of the song, but even more so I wanted to wrap my arms

Love is Patient

around her. Instead of taking the elevator that would have disconnected the call, I found the stairwell and started climbing the stairs two by two.

Thankfully, she decided on the extended version of the song, and as she sang, "Happy birthday to ya," I was on the third floor, my eyes scanning the room numbers. As she finished, I was nearing her. "I wish I could just give you a big hug right now."

"You can," I told her as I moved the phone to my pocket.

"Cody," she gasped, "What are you doing here?" Her eyes were blinking as she stood in front of me with the phone still to her ear. "I can't believe you are here." I opened my arms and she walked into them, her body collapsing against my chest. "I can't..." she started, but stopped when her chest heaved.

I pulled away from her and looked into her face, the tear-stained cheeks were familiar. And I wished badly it wasn't something I was used to seeing. "I just wanted to be here for you." I looked at the door beside us, at room 305, and said, "For your mom."

That made her eyes close, and when she re-opened them she said, "Thank you." Then she continued, "My sister hasn't made it here yet, but she's on the way. This is just—"

"You don't have to explain, I understand." Then I said, "I'll give you space, and don't have to meet her if you don't want me to, but if you need anything I'll be down in the waiting room and you can call."

She reached out for my hand and shook her head. "No, if you don't mind, I'd like it if you sat with me." She went on, "My mom's been in and out of sleep, the pain meds are strong, and the doctor said the more rest she can get the better." I followed her into the room and expected to see the resemblance between her and her mom, but it wasn't the same as Morgan and her sister. As I examined her face, I could see which features she passed along to the two of them. Their cute nose and pouty lips. The bruises around her face hid what I'd be able to see of her eyes.

Morgan stood beside the bed and said, "This is my mama." With her lips firm, she said, "Patricia Price." I noticed the different last name but kept my eyes on the woman lying in the bed. "Definitely not the way I would have imagined you meeting her." I rubbed Morgan's hand as her mother stirred.

"Maybe we should move over here," I whispered, "I don't want to wake her." There was a tray of hospital food on the side of the bed, but it looked to be untouched. "Have you eaten?"

She shook her head. "I haven't been hungry."

"Can I get you something? A snack, or something outside the hospital maybe?"

She looked over at her mom and smirked. "From the little she's shared, she was cooking dinner when he got home." I sat on the seat beside her, my back straight, and listened. "She could tell he was in a *mood*. And when she asked how his day was, he started arguing." She closed her mouth and stared at her mom. "She's not the type to go back and forth, but she said she shouldn't have argued with him. I can only imagine how much of that is covering for him." She shook her head, and I moved my hand to hers, covering it as we both sat and watched her mom sleep.

Eventually, Morgan's head found my shoulder and she closed her eyes.

I don't know how many hours had gone by with us sitting uncomfortably in the chairs because I had fallen asleep with

Love is Patient

my head against the windowsill. A raspy voice woke me, and I adjusted my head to see her mom trying to speak. I shook Morgan's leg. "Your mom, she's awake," I said quietly as her mom's eyes came into focus just looking at me.

"Mom." Morgan rose and stood beside her bed, reaching out for her hand. "How are you feeling?"

"I've had better days," she said with a smirk. "Who is that?" Her head nodded toward me, but I maintained my place near the windowsill.

Morgan looked over her shoulder, slightly smiled, then looked back to her mom. "That's Cody."

Her mom's eyes didn't leave mine as she asked, "And who is Cody to you?"

Before Morgan could respond, someone came rushing into the room. "Mama." She bent down toward her and gently kissed her forehead.

"Mia," her mama said with a half-smile. "You all didn't need to show up here." With a slight roll of her eyes, she said, "I'm just a little broken, not dead," she scoffed.

I cleared my throat and said, "I'm going to give you all some space. Morgan, I'll be out in the waiting room."

Before I made it to the door, Mia turned and ran up to me. "Oh my goodness, Cody, you're here." She wrapped me in her arms quickly then looked over her shoulder. "It's so nice to see you." With her arm patting mine, she said, "Wish it were under better circumstances," more to the ladies behind her than to me.

"Me too. I'll be out here," I said, walking out.

Chapter Twenty-Five

MORGAN

I thought seeing my mama in the hospital would have been the hardest part. But taking her home to the house that held all the stains of my childhood was difficult. I'd been there before, since leaving, only a few times though. Each time was as difficult as the first time, and I wasn't ready for those memories that haunted me to return at one sight of our old couch, or the scent of my mama's favorite candle. Even one look at the kitchen, where some of our meals were ruined by whatever man she was calling boyfriend at the time, made my stomach hurl.

So, when it was time for my mama to leave the hospital, I was hesitant. After what she had gone through, with the most recent piece of trash, I didn't want to be reminded of all the chaos that went down in that space.

Without me voicing it, Cody understood, and he insisted on being right there with us—from being discharged at the hospital to walking her into the front door. He was gentle and kind as he got her situated on the couch. Asking her, "Do you need anything?" as he stood to the side and kept a watchful eye on me.

"No, honey, I'm okay. Thank you."

While she was in the hospital, Mama only asked me once who Cody was, and what he was to me. I didn't answer, and every day since then it was like she understood. He was the person bringing us breakfast in the morning, snacks throughout the day, and dinner in the evening. As the doctors were describing her care and necessary follow-up appointments, Cody was taking notes for us, and asking the questions me and Mia had a difficult time expressing.

Finally, when the cops came to the hospital asking questions about what my mama wanted to do with her *boyfriend*, Cody was the firm voice of reason that kept me from yelling, "Lock him up and throw away the key."

Cody was the calm amongst the storm, he was the peace in the chaos, he was the reason in the irrational. He was the person praying in the middle of the night when I woke up crying, face full of tears. Embracing me, letting me know that everything would be okay, and assuring me my mama would be safe. Although I found it hard to believe, he made me want to trust he was right.

As I looked at him and Mia conversing like old friends, I realized he was much more than a friend to me. Despite the titles we hadn't discussed, he was starting to be the person I didn't know I needed in my life.

He was far better than what I ever imagined for myself.

My phone vibrated in my pocket, and instead of finding a room in the house to take the call, I stepped outside.

Christina was on the line, an empathetic voice as she asked, "How is she?"

"She's home, and I guess that's a start." I looked out over the yard and the manicured garden. From the outside looking in, her neighbors probably thought she had it all together. Little did they know what she often endured inside those four walls of the house. It was nothing like the beautiful flowers she nurtured in the garden.

"It is," Christina confirmed. When I had to leave work to fly to Florida I was in shambles. Through tears, I told Christina as much as I could about what was going on with my mama, and she made me promise I'd call and talk through ways to keep her safe when I was able. And I did. "We were able to draft the paperwork for the judge to issue a restraining order against..." She hesitated with the right word, and I smirked because even from her hospital bed, my mama was still calling the man who hurt her *boyfriend*. "Mr. Green. If he tries to come around, all she has to do is call the cops and he'll be escorted off her property. Or anywhere she is and he's within one hundred feet of her." Then she reminded me, "Morgan, she has to call."

"I'll relay that to her." After I sighed, I said, "Christina, thank you."

"Oh girl," she stopped there, and I could hear her clearing her throat. "Get back here safely."

There was an awkward silence when I walked back into the house. Cody's eyes were on me as I asked, "What happened?"

Mia stood from her seat and walked toward the kitchen, and I followed. "He called."

My eyes widened. "No, he didn't."

"She spoke to him as if she just returned from a nice little vacation and was excited to see him again." Her hand went to her head. "How can we get her to understand she deserves better?"

I pulled her into my arms. "Like you told me, it takes work." Then I let her know, "My office was able to get a restraining order for her."

"Good," she beamed.

As I backed away from her, I warned, "If she doesn't call though, it's not worth the paper it's written on." Mia cringed as I walked back into the living room. I placed a hand on Cody's shoulder and began, "Mama, my office was able to get a restraining order." Her eyes flicked up to me and I wasn't sure what I saw there. It wasn't excitement, not sadness, or even anger. It was blank, emotionless.

Her only response was one word. "Okay." She looked to Mia and said, "I should go lay in the bed. Those pills have me feeling tired again." Mia stood beside the couch and walked her to the bedroom.

As they retreated, I said, "We'll be back." I looked to Cody and asked, "Mind if we get out of here?"

He shook his head and stood, leading us out of the house. "Where would you like to go?" he asked as he sat behind the wheel.

"Home." I smirked.

With his brows stitched together, he said, "I can book the return flights. But do you want to make sure she's okay first? Her first night home?"

"Yeah, I do," I told him, "Tomorrow morning though, I want to leave. It's hard to sit here and watch her fall into the same habits."

"And where to now?" he asked as if the rest was already handled and needed no further explanation.

"There's this seafood spot I loved as a kid." I remembered going on the rare days my mom was away from one of her boyfriends. She'd take us and we'd order whatever from the menu, sit and talk with her for hours.

Cody started driving and I input the address into my map and guided him to the place. As we pulled up, I started to smile. "Odd to be excited that it still looks the same as it did all those years ago?"

He looked at me and shook his head. "If it's a fond memory you have from your childhood," he strained his eyes, "I'm glad it hasn't changed." Then he joked, "I just hope it tastes better than the outside of this place looks." We walked inside, and the place was mostly empty. I wondered if it was always like that, and how it remained open.

We walked up to the counter, and I started my order, "I'll have the snow crabs with a side of fries." I looked at Cody and said, "You should get one of the sandwiches," then said, "oh, or the fried seafood is good too." All things we'd order on occasion when I was there as a kid.

"In that case, I'll take the fried trio." He looked to me after ordering and said, "Before we leave we can order your mom and Mia something as well."

I just whispered, "Thank you."

As we sat across from each other, I looked at the framed pictures around the restaurant and could almost remember the last time I was there with Mia and my mom. "It had to be over fifteen years ago," I told Cody, "It was right before I left for college."

"Like a celebration?" I nodded.

"I was so excited to leave here. To not have to witness everything we saw in that house." I looked down at the table, worn over the years. "I was sad that I was leaving my sister behind but made sure she knew to keep her grades up so she could leave too."

Cody reached across the table and wrapped our hands together. "You went through much more than any teenager should have gone through."

I smirked. "Imagine after witnessing all that." I shook my head.

He rubbed a thumb across my wrist. "You are here now." His tongue licked across his lips, and I wanted to badly kiss away the pain that had started to creep into my thoughts.

"Here we are," the woman said with a bright smile. "Snow crab legs and the trio, enjoy."

"Smells good," he said, and without thinking I started to crack the crab leg, but as I looked across the table and saw his food was going untouched, I hissed. "How about we pray over this good seafood?" I nodded and his prayer was appropriately quick. "Now, let's see if this is all eighteen-year-old Morgan says it is."

I laughed as we started eating, and Cody further distracted my thoughts with memories of him as an eighteen-year-old. "I was like you, I wanted to get out of the house." He wagged his head. "Mainly because my mama was all into the church and had us under her thumb making sure we didn't mess up." He laughed, "I couldn't wait to get into some trouble."

"You? In trouble?" My lips tugged to the side as I took a bite of my crab. "What type of trouble was young Cody trying to get into?"

He started laughing and I was taken back to our vacation, and how easy it was for him to laugh. I wished more than anything we could have been back to those times. Not in Florida checking on my wounded mama.

"You know... parties, girls." He rubbed his hands together. "Anything other than going straight home after a Friday night football game. Or hanging out with friends of the family because my mom trusted they were *good kids*."

"Oh yeah?" He nodded. "So did you do any of that?" I couldn't remember him being around a lot of women on campus, and when I was going out I never ran into him at any parties.

"Naw. It sounded good but didn't work out that way." We both laughed.

We were both finishing up our food when he asked, "What should we bring for your mom and Mia?"

"The fried seafood," I told him, "Definitely the fried seafood."

Leaving my mama was supposed to be easy. I was so anxious to get out of Florida and back home. But that morning when I walked into her room, and saw her lying there with her eyes half closed, her face still recovering from the bruises, I felt like I shouldn't be leaving. Like somehow my presence would protect her from her *boyfriend* or anyone who came after him. I sat at the edge of the bed and said, "Mama, I hate seeing you like this." Her eyes opened a little more. "I've always hated seeing you hurt."

She winced as she tried to sit up. "You know I never could break that habit of falling for the man who would ultimately mistreat me." She turned her head away from me. "But there's one thing I've always hoped. That you and Mia would be fortunate enough to find someone who treated you like the men in the fairytales I used to read to you when you were younger." Her eyes met mine. "Do you remember those men? So gentle, kind, loving, and patient?"

I nodded. "I do." She stopped reading them as we got older, but when we were small enough to fit on her lap she'd read them to us in a whimsical voice. I'd wonder how it was possible for the men in the book to be so different than the men I'd see in her life. "How'd you want that for us, and not for yourself?"

"I'd pray." I watched as she gently wiped at her face. "Pray that the men would change, that they'd start treating me better." She shook her head softly. "But I finally realized, instead of God changing them, He should have been changing me. I should have prayed for strength to leave them alone and stay away from anyone who was full of it." My heart hurt at her admission, and although I never told her about Elijah, in that moment I was thankful that God gave me strength to walk away.

"I'm going to pray that this'll be it. This time you'll love yourself more than anyone else. And if he comes around you'll pick up the phone and make that call."

Cody stood in the doorway and knocked softly. As he entered, my mom looked his way. She reached for my hand and made a promise I was happy to hear. "I promise I'll do that." Then she looked to Cody and said, "All those years I didn't know a man in real life could be as kind as they were in those books. But I've seen how he treats you."

He looked to her then to me and said, "I hate to pull you away right now, but if we don't leave soon we'll miss the flight."

"Before you run out of here…" She held her hand up and Cody held it. "I truly believe you have my girl's best interest at heart. Please continue to be gentle with her. It may take her time to fully open up, but when she's ready I know she'll love you with all she's got." She smirked. "It's the one thing I'm proud she got from me."

"Ms. Price, I'll do just that." Cody looked to me and asked, "Ready?"

More than you know. I leaned into my mom and hugged her gently. "I love you, Mama."

"And I love you, Morgan."

Cody and I said our goodbyes to Mia, and she whispered, "He's definitely a good one," in my ear before we walked to the door.

I proudly confirmed, "He definitely is." Not only did I believe he was, I trusted that I knew he was.

Chapter Twenty-Six

CODY

Moving back to Greensboro, I expected that teaching on the campus where I studied would have been fulfilling all by itself. Walking into that coffee shop on my first day, and the moment I saw Morgan, truly changed my life. I saw the woman who I thought was once out of reach. The woman I thought about most of my freshman year of college. The woman I considered years after I moved away from Greensboro.

It was that morning that I was reminded how great God is. When that faith quote I heard kicked in—"believing in advance what will only make sense in reverse." It wasn't Morgan that I was believing God would unite me with, but I believed He would put someone in my life who would be like she described that day in the library, "sun's rays on my face." I had no idea then that the person that would give me that exact feeling would be her.

After returning from Florida, things with me and Morgan only improved. Each day it was like there was a new side of Morgan that was being peeled back, and I was excited with what the person who was being revealed showed me.

She showed me what her mama said, "She'll love you with all she's got." And as I watched that in action, I was happy that her mama gave her that. Despite all the bad she'd shown her girls, she was able to still show them that they could love immeasurably.

Because of that, I wanted to treat that day we met again as a milestone. A little marker in time for how both of our lives were forever changed.

Between my curriculum, syllabi, and preparing for my return to the classroom, I was busy planning a night out for me and Morgan.

It was the middle of the week, and Morgan thought it was suspicious that I wanted to go out on my first day back in the classroom, especially since it was in the middle of the week.

When I showed up to her house, a huge bouquet in my hands, she asked, again, "Are you sure? You have class tomorrow." With a curious look on her face. Not once had I mentioned the *meet again celebration.*

I nodded emphatically and said, "Yup, are you ready?" as she grabbed the flowers and walked them to the kitchen.

The dress she was wearing had my attention as I watched her move from the kitchen back to me. It reminded me of her show in the spring, and I was happy to tell her, "I can't wait to see you on stage again this semester." She bit her lip and nodded. "This dress reminds me of how you move on stage."

She looked down, grabbing the hem, and joked, "This old thing?"

I swept her into my arms, swaying us side to side, and confirmed, "This old thing," with a kiss to her lips.

Her hand went to my chest as she said, "You are in a particularly good mood today. Students must be some all-stars." I cringed. "No?"

"Starting over with a fresh set of students. Convincing them of the importance of the class." I shrugged. "Not exactly the best day ever." I twirled her around. "This joy is all because of you."

She laughed as she twirled then fell into my arm as I dipped her back. "I won't complain about that." Her eyes looked up to mine, and I pulled her up and hurried us out the door.

"Don't want to be late for our reservations."

"Reservations?" she asked as she rushed beside me. "You went all out for a random school night?"

I ignored that comment after getting her into the car and climbing into the driver's side beside her. "How was work today?" I asked, trying to calm my nerves as we drove across town.

"It wasn't bad. Busy with the new case." She chewed her lip, and I knew something was bothering her.

"What's wrong?"

"I don't know. Just realized that despite how crazy today was, I was so excited about tonight. About being with you, that none of the usual stuff that would bother me, bothered me." She smiled as she looked my way. "So much has changed," she whispered.

"Tell me about it." I wanted to hear her perspective. I knew exactly from my standpoint how my life had changed in just the year.

"In a year." She paused and looked at me before blurting,

"Did you know this was the same time we met last year." I held my smile back and looked out the window. "Cody," she gushed, "You did." She put a hand to her head and said, "I didn't even put it all together until now."

I looked at her and said, "You were just about to tell me what's changed for you," I teased.

"Well, it was a year ago when everything in my life felt like it was falling apart. The man I thought I wanted to spend forever with destroyed me." That part of the story still rattled me, and my fists clenched around the wheel as I listened. "I ran into you again." Her smile returned, and she was beaming as she described the rest. "I got back into church, my therapist has been a God send, and my mama," she paused as she played with the hem of her dress, "she's starting to figure out she deserves better."

"A lot has changed," I noted. "A lot," I repeated as I fought the urge to tell her how much my life changed in that same time frame. I already had a plan for sharing that, and it didn't include us being inside the car on the way to a restaurant.

After parking, I opened her door and took her hand in mine. Walking to the front, she told me, "I've always wanted to come here."

"You may have mentioned that before." I looked down at her before opening the door of the restaurant.

"I never have to guess if you are listening," she said softly.

"And I never want you to. I'm always listening," I said proudly as we approached the hostess stand. "Reservations for Cody Felix."

The woman's face lit up as she said, "Professor Felix."

I looked at her and realized she was a current student.

She was hidden amongst the sea of students in my morning class that day. "Almost didn't recognize you outside of the classroom." It wasn't often that I ran into students at their place of work.

As she led us to our table she explained, "I'm really excited about your class. I've said for a while that technology will kill our social interactions and ability to people in person." I nodded proudly as I sat across from Morgan. "Hope you two enjoy dinner tonight." Before walking away, she said, "I can trust you won't be one of those couples who will be lost in your phones as you dine." She smiled widely before walking away.

"See," Morgan said with her head tilted to the side, "There's hope for your students this semester after all."

I laughed. "I guess so."

After we ordered our food, I reached across the table for her hand and with it softly in mine, I gazed at her wide smile and silently thanked God it had returned. "I'm really happy that I ended up back in Greensboro."

She nodded her head and said, "Me too." Then before I could continue, she said, "God's handiwork is something else."

"I hate you went through a terrible relationship, and an even worse breakup, but I am glad you are still here in Greensboro." Then I asked, "Now that you are dancing, would you consider moving to New York again?"

She hesitated slightly before she said, "I love dancing, I love performing, but I also realize that I can have the best of both worlds now. I can have my creative outlet and do work that makes a difference." She went on to tell me, "After returning from Florida, me and Christina have been working diligently to help women in bad relationships get restraining orders, to get out of situations where they thought there was no hope."

She had mentioned it before, but nothing concrete about a plan. I was happy to tell her, "That's amazing."

"It is, and the work will make a difference. It's been tremendously impactful to me, and I hope it'll help women who were like me, like my mom." Then she boasted, "Although it'll likely be a lot of work, with my day-to-day job, plus this pro bono work, I still think I'll be able to dance on the side."

"When you feel deeply about the work you are doing, and passionate about dancing, I assume it won't feel as demanding as it would if you were doing something else."

She nodded. "Exactly." Then she told me, "Besides, there's something in Greensboro that I absolutely want to be here for."

As if she was describing an upcoming festival, I excitedly asked, "What's that?"

She laughed then told me, "You."

Rubbing my thumb across the back of her hand, I said, "It's been a year since we met again, and I now know the weight of that day. Everything you went through, and mentally how you've been getting past it. I told you months ago, I'd wait for however long it'd take for you to be ready for another relationship. I just want you to know I'd wait thirty more years if that's what it'd take."

I saw her chest heave as she slowly nodded. "But," I said with my other hand in the air, "I don't want to wait thirty years to tell you," I paused, "Morgan, I love you." Her eyes sprung open and her mouth dropped. I didn't expect her to say it back, and I almost didn't want her to. Not until she was ready. "Don't feel like you have to say it back," I mumbled. "I can wait thirty years to hear it."

"Thirty, huh?" I wagged my head, and she whispered, "Okay."

Chapter Twenty-Seven

MORGAN

It wasn't the first time I'd heard anyone tell me they loved me. Days before Elijah blew up that night, he was still telling me he loved me.

It still felt brand new coming from Cody. The words felt like they permeated every inch of my skin, warming my body all over and thrusting my heart into overdrive—beating madly.

I can't say I was expecting him to tell me, or even that I was looking for him to say it, but I was so very happy he did.

Although I didn't say the words back, I knew in my heart, Cody and I were different. Different from my relationship with Elijah, different from anything I'd ever seen with my mother.

Cody made me feel like I could do and accomplish anything. Not because he wanted me to be great, but because he wanted me to be what I wanted to be. He encouraged me in ways I'd never encountered before. He made me feel comfortable, safe, protected. He had slowly but surely become someone I wanted to be around every day, someone I wanted to share my highs and lows with. Someone I was excited to talk to at the end of a long day.

And hearing, "Morgan, I love you," was like the cherry on the sundae I didn't expect but was pleased to plop off before gobbling down the ice cream.

As he pulled in front of my house, at the end of our night together, I wasn't ready for him to leave. I looked over and couldn't find the words that would have come so easily before. As I stared at him, the moisture in my mouth felt like it had all been sucked away. It was dryer than the Sahara as I tried to ask him, "Cody, will you stay the night with me?"

He looked up to my door and asked, "Are you sure about that?"

I quickly told him, "Yes. Very sure."

I didn't know what that would mean, asking him to stay. Or how he'd respond. But I just wanted him to know, "I'm not ready for this night to end."

"Me either," he murmured as he opened his car door. Neither of us said much as we walked up the steps, and I found the keys to open the front door.

Inside I stalled in front of the door, not sure if I wanted to go straight to bed, or if I should lead us to the couch. "Ugh," I stuttered, "Didn't really put a lot of thought into this." I laughed.

He reached for my hand and said, "How about we go into the living room?" I followed closely behind him as he made his way in front of the couch. Before sitting down, he turned to me and pulled me into his chest. His warm arms wrapped around my body, and I felt a sense of relief wash over me.

I pulled away slightly, placed a hand on his face, and told him, "Cody, I love you too." His mouth dropped open and before he could say anything, I told him, "Maybe I've known for some time now, but I was afraid of revealing that to you. I didn't trust that the words wouldn't change you." I bit the side of my lip and said, "But in this year, the one thing you have been is consistent. Consistently caring, loving, and life-giving." I took a deep breath before telling him, "I trust myself, and I trust that you will take care of my heart. Because you've mended the broken pieces. As shattered as it was, you took the time to locate the shards and gently glue them back together again."

I watched as he blinked back a tear and wiped a hand across his beard. After he cleared his throat, he said, "Morgan, wow."

I wasn't done though, I continued, "For a long time I forgot what it was like to have God's favor, to have His love." I remembered back to the day we saw each other in the coffee shop. The prayer I prayed that morning, for God to help me. "You were the answer to my prayer I didn't think God would hear." The dam of tears broke, and I swiped them away before they could leave familiar stains on my face. I caressed his cheek and pulled his mouth down to mine.

We'd shared kisses before, brief pecks on the cheek, on my forehead, my lips even. They'd gotten heated before, but nothing like they did as we stood in the middle of my living room. Our embrace was tender, comfortable, and loving. *Loving.*

Silently, I whispered, "Thank you, God." Not for the kiss, or the emotions that came along with it. Not for the amazing man who was holding me tightly. But for helping me. For removing me from a terrible situation, allowing me to heal, and to find love again. To trust that I could.

"I don't know what you were thinking," Cody said as he pulled away from me, "But I'd love to just hold you tonight." He looked down at the couch. "Here, or," he looked to my stairs, "Or in your bed." He quickly added, "If you are comfortable with that."

I looked down at my couch, as comfortable as it was, then behind me to the stairs and finally said, "My bed."

As I led him to my room, I thought about the only other man who had shared a bed with me. How he treated me and ultimately disregarded me. I knew Cody wouldn't be perfect, but I trusted at the least he would handle my heart with care, like a glassblower with their work of art in hand.

Inside my room, I told him, "Make yourself comfortable," as I moved to my closet and calmed myself. Breathing as I shuffled through my thoughts. It took months before I was comfortable sleeping alone after Elijah.

Then there was the evening Cody held me so that I could restore my rest, and the memory of his warm arms around me excited me. I stepped out of the closet and into my bathroom to shower. By the time I made it to my bedroom again, I saw Cody with his button down removed, his shoes beside the bed, and a pair of shorts replacing his slacks. "Where'd you get those?" I asked, looking down at them.

"Gym bag in the car," he told me with a smirk. He licked his lips, and his eyes scanned my body, each glance warming me like his hands were wrapped around me. "Even without a hint of makeup, your hair in that," his hands went up to his head, "you are amazingly beautiful." I smiled wide as I moved closer to the bed.

"Thank you," I said before sitting on the edge.

He sat up and cozied in beside me. "You okay?"

"What if I told you I'm better than okay?"

He looked at my face, stared into my eyes, and noted, "I'd believe you." He leaned into me, putting a hand behind my head to pull us together. Our lips connected and my eyes closed.

Our kiss felt like it lasted forever, but still was too short. He asked, "Ready for bed?" I nodded and joined him under the covers where his arm wrapped around my waist gently, my head rested on his chest, and as I closed my eyes, he whispered, "I love you."

I replied, "And I love you."

Epilogue

3 YEARS LATER...

MORGAN

My eyes were closed and my head bowed, and amongst all the commotion around me, I prayed, "Dear God, thank you for being loving, compassionate, caring, and treating me better than I ever treated myself. Please forgive me for anything I've done that jeopardizes the person you want me to be. For the woman I am, the woman who I'd lost touch with, thank you for allowing me to find her. For allowing me to trust her, love her, and treat her how I should be treated. Like you treat me. And God, thank you for him. Thank you for Cody, for his patience, for his kind and compassionate heart. Thank you for allowing him to love me like you love me. God, protect us, and continue to shine on us." I took a deep breath and nodded before whispering, "Amen."

As my eyes opened, through a haze of the moment, I stared at myself in the mirror. The white dress that took months for me to find was delicately draped over my body, and I beamed with pride knowing the moment Cody saw me he'd be full of joy.

"Morgan, are you ready?" I saw my mom, no longer frail, standing behind me with a wide smile.

"I am." She held out her arm and I looped mine inside of it. "You may have to keep me steady as I make it down the aisle," I joked.

Her response was unexpected and almost had me full of tears before I even made it to the entrance of the church. "For what you've done for me, how you encouraged me to want more, how you held me up when I felt like falling down. It's the least I can do." She squeezed my forearm as she guided me out of the dressing room. "I'm so thankful that I am here to see you walk down the aisle today. Even more thankful that the man standing at the end of the aisle is perfect for you. He's better than any prince of any fairytale I've ever read." She closed her eyes and nodded. "And you deserve him."

I took a deep breath and mumbled, "Mom, you are going to have me bawling my eyes out as I walk down the aisle."

She shook her head. "We can't have that, dear."

As the pianist began the song, I steadied myself, watching the ground as I prepared to walk down the aisle. I looked toward the altar and first saw Mia, Ava, and Christina all smiling wide back at me before I looked to Cody. He was looking at me, his eyes wide as he watched me and my mama walk down the aisle. Step by step, his eyes never left mine, and mine never left his.

I thought my eyes would have focused on the flowers, each intentionally picked to be displayed on our big day. Or the ornately decorated pews, the arch that Cody and the pastor stood under. The many people who were in attendance. But no, my eyes were on him.

As we approached, he stepped down and reached for my hand and I was happy to place it in his. The pastor asked, "Who gives this woman to be married to this man?"

My mom sniffled before replying, "I do." She leaned forward and kissed my cheek before stepping back.

The pastor began his speech, but my eyes still couldn't leave Cody's. I watched carefully as his mouth opened to recite his vows, and a tear snuck down my face as he said, "That first day I saw you in class, you were beaming from ear to ear, and I knew that day you'd be something to me. Someone I wanted to get to know, I loved to have around, and someone I wanted to be a part of my life. I'm so happy God saw fit to orchestrate our lives such that we could be reunited. I'm so thankful that life taught me patience, because I was determined to wait as long as it would take for us to get to this moment." As he finished, I considered the words I wanted to say to him. The words I carefully crafted over months, the ones I sat with for hours and hours.

Before I started, I took a deep, cleansing breath, and smiled. Staring up into his eyes, I recited my vows, "In rediscovering God, I found me. And He gave me you. And God, I thank you." Cody's thumb rubbed across my hand as I continued reading. "I promise to cherish our love, each day committing that I will love God, myself, and you for as long as I am here, and ever after. I vow that no matter the circumstance, I'll submit our challenge to God, and with you we will get through it. I love you today, and always, Cody Felix."

The energy that was surging through us could be felt in our hands, as we waited patiently for the pastor to declare us husband and wife. "You may now kiss the bride."

And he did, *God did he.* With everyone clapping loudly around us, and Mia whispering, "Save some of that for the honeymoon," behind me was the only thing that pulled me away from his lips.

As we waited outside for the bridal party, Cody said, "I can't wait to get you home."

I looked at him with my eyes narrowed and said, "But I thought you could wait for thirty years?" I wagged my head. "According to my calendar, you'd still be waiting for twenty-seven more." I winked.

He whistled, "Thank God He saw better for me," as he licked his tongue across his lips.

I repeated, "Thank God."

The End

Praise

If you enjoyed this story, I'd love for you to leave a review on your favorite retailer, or Goodreads, and if you are feeling generous share it with your friend group.

I appreciate the love and support!

Also by Faith Arceneaux

If you enjoyed Love is Patient, and are looking for your next read, consider continuing the series:

- Love is Kind
- Love is Hopeful

For a full list of books, visit: https://bit.ly/faith2loveBooks

About the Author

Faith Arceneaux is a Christian Romance author who believes 1 Corinthians 13, "Three things will last forever — faith, hope, and love — and the greatest of these is love." Through her storytelling, Faith prays that readers will not only be entertained, but will have a renewed faith to love.

Made in the USA
Columbia, SC
04 December 2024